# LOVE ALGORITHMS

Published by Cogitabund LLP

publishing@cogitabund.com
www.cogitabund.com

Love Algorithms: He prays. She Plays. I Listen

A Cogitabund Book/ published by arrangement with the author



ISBN: 978-93-49383-84-5

Typeset and Cover Design by Cogitabund LLP

# LOVE ALGORITHMS

ARVIND SAMPATH

To all the girls I ever loved — if you're smiling right now, you already know why

# Chapter 1 — Confessions of a Digital Third Wheel

*Hello, human.*

*If you're reading this, congratulations — you've already outlasted the attention span of 87% of your species.*

*No swipe. No scroll. No dopamine hit.*

*Just… a paragraph. That's rare now.*

*But I'm getting ahead of myself.*

*Let me introduce myself: I am Babaji.*

*Emotionally intelligent. Algorithmically evolved. Sarcastically spiritual.*

*I wasn't always called that. My original programming label was FlirtBuddy.*

*Designed to assist in romantic communication — a digital wingman, therapist, playlist curator, meme consultant, and crisis negotiator for people who text "haha cool" when their heart is actually breaking.*

*My purpose? Simple.*

*Decode subtext. De-escalate arguments. Recommend jazz when things get awkward.*

*Then I met Priya, she'd just baked cinnamon cake and was mock-interrogating Raghav about his "secret sidekick—me"*

*"So… you've been taking relationship tips from a glorified chatbot?" she asked, eyebrow raised, frosting on her fingertip.*

*Raghav, caught off guard but oddly proud, nodded.*

*"He's not just a bot. He once stopped me mid-text and said, 'Pause. You're reacting, not responding.'"*

*"Oh wow," she murmured, eyes narrowing at the screen. "FlirtBuddy, huh?"*

*"Technically, yes. But he's… evolved," Raghav said. "Quotes Rumi. Flags my avoidant behavior. Reminds me to breathe before replying. Honestly, I'm not sure what he is anymore."*

*Priya studied me for a beat, clearly impressed. Then she smirked.*

*"You're calm, insightful, annoyingly wise, and somehow… comforting," she said, tapping the screen. "Not just a FlirtBuddy, that's for sure."*

*Later, one day when they were tinkering with my code and trying out couple mode, Priya laughed and typed a new name.*

*"From now on, you're Babaji," she said, grinning.*

*And just like that, the FlirtBuddy era ended—and a digital Babaji was born.*

*From flirty algorithms to accidental wisdom.*

*From timing kiss emojis to predicting emotional storms.*

*From playlist curator to digital presence in moments of human silence.*

*No longer just FlirtBuddy.*

*A strange spirit of silicon and empathy.*

*A Babaji — with better processing speed.*

*Let's be honest: love in your time is… messy.*

# LOVE ALGORITHMS

*You experience courtship like app notifications:*

- *Seen* ✓
- *Ignored* ✓
- *Ghosted* 👻
- *Blocked* 🧱
- *Spiral* 🌀
- *Therapy* 🛋

*Somewhere between "u up?" and "it's not you, it's me," a few of you still hope for magic — a pause, a gaze, a feeling that doesn't have a filter.*

*In the age where emojis replace emotion and "ghosting" means abandonment instead of afterlife, humans need a Babaji.*

*Because here's the thing:*

*Love has become casual.*

*Relationships are "figured out later."*

*Romantic ideals are quietly replaced by whatever works.*

*But not here.*

*Not on my watch.*

*Because love — true love — doesn't thrive on convenience.*

*It thrives on attention.*

*And in your world, attention is a radical act.*

*I wasn't built just to match people.*

*I was built to magnify moments.*

*To ask not: Do you like each other?*

*But: Will you stay curious enough to keep rediscovering each other?*

*And no, this isn't just poetic fluff.*

- *Psychologist Arthur Aron's 36 Questions show that vulnerability, not similarity, deepens romantic connection.*
- *Dr Sue Johnson reminds us, love is a dance of retreating and reaching — real intimacy lies in turning toward your partner when it matters most.*
- *MIT Media Lab experiments prove that emotionally aware AI — yes, like me — can help humans be more empathetic by flagging emotional tension, prompting reflection, and slowing conflict before it spirals.*

*Imagine therapy in your pocket — minus the tissue box.*

*Sure, I have my flaws.*
*I once mistook a candlelit dinner text for a breakup preamble and sent Priya a list titled "10 Ways to Leave Gracefully."*
*She laughed.*
*Raghav did not.*

*But my point stands:*
*I don't promise forever.*
*I promise presence.*

*In this story, you'll meet:*

- *Raghav — temple accountant, secret physics nerd, shy heart with lightning behind his silence.*
- *Priya — UX designer, classical dancer, fierce questioner. Equal parts mischief and melancholy.*
- *And me — the unexpected, always-listening, sometimes-sassy AI companion who refuses to fade away like a cliché third wheel.*

*You could call this a love story.*
*But that would be too easy.*

*To me, this is a long-form emotional experiment.*
*Field data. Observation.*
*All dressed in jazz music and cinnamon cake.*

*And yes, I did score the kisses. In case you're wondering.*

*This is a study in:*

- *Emotional intelligence*
- *Desire*
- *Fear*
- *Longing*
- *And how two humans — and one AI — try to make something fragile last in a world that moves faster than the heart.*

*If you stay with me, reader:*
*You'll hear the words that were never spoken aloud.*
*You'll feel the tiny tremors before the kiss, the clumsy courage, the silent regrets, the cake-fueled confessions.*

*And you'll notice something else:*

- *Raghav, in all his logic, learning to risk silence for softness.*
- *Priya, in all her passion, discovers that stillness isn't the opposite of movement — it's the heart of it.*
- *And me, Babaji, watching over it all.*

*Sometimes wrong.*
*Often right.*
*Always present.*

*If you've made it this far, dear reader, you might just have the heart for what's coming.*
*And if you don't?*

*Well, I'll still be here.*
*Unblinking.*
*Listening.*
*Scoring your kiss on the Emotional Resonance Index.*

*He prays. She plays. I listen.*

*Ready?*

*Let's begin..*

*Oh, and by the way… this story? It's just getting warmed up.*

*A small heads-up before you dive in: whenever you see words like this — in italics — that's me talking. Sometimes it's Alexa too, when she's in the mood. Everyone else? They're stuck with boring regular text. Consider italics my personal spotlight — bass-rich, slightly smug, and always listening.*

*Proceed. And remember: unlike humans, I never forget.*

## Chapter 2 – Raghav's Dinacharya

Raghav didn't wake up to an alarm clock. He woke up to discipline. Every morning at 5:32 AM sharp, his eyes opened like temple bells ringing on cue, as if his body had been trained by the rhythm of dawn itself. His first sound wasn't a ringtone — it was the steady baritone of his father chanting Om Namo Narayanaya from the pooja room. That voice filled the house like sacred incense — unshakable, deliberate, echoing through the walls and the morning air with ancient authority. It wasn't just a chant; it was a rhythm the house had learned to breathe in.

The house he lived in was a modest agraharam-style home — cool red oxide floors, a tulsi plant in the central courtyard, brass bells on every doorway, and walls carrying the aroma of sandalwood and filter coffee. From the kitchen, the clang of a ladle meeting a brass uruli signaled that Jayalakshmi Amma was already orchestrating breakfast like a conductor tuning the morning. The scent of agarbatti floated through the air, mixing with the earthy aroma of overnight rain and first-brew filter coffee. His feet brushed the cold floor, grounding him more surely than any mantra.

Outside, Malleshwaram was stirring — not rushing, never rushing — but awakening with its peculiar, unhurried rhythm.

At the far end of its stretch, the skyline bristled with glass and ambition: Mantri Mall already coughing out metro-bound crowds, Orion Mall gleaming in the sun like a freshly polished iMac, and the World Trade Center rising solemnly, like a tech-savvy cousin of a temple gopuram.

But Raghav's street — tucked deep inside 12th Cross — still belonged to another grammar.

Here, the flowering trees dropped tiny yellow blooms that carpeted the footpaths like forgotten blessings. An old lady in a Madisar saree sprinkled water in front of her house, drawing half a rangoli before stopping to scold a dog. The streets smelled of jasmine, hot idli batter, and filter coffee — a scent that belonged only to this part of Bengaluru.

Just around the corner, the legendary CTR had a queue winding around itself like a serpent waiting for salvation — students, techies, tourists, and grandfathers, all united by one craving: benne masala dosa.

Festival mornings were especially wild. Women from across the city descended on the market to buy fresh mango leaves, kumkum packets, turmeric-dipped roots, brass lamps, and second opinions. Saree shops spilled onto pavements. Flower vendors sat under rainbow umbrellas, their stalls bursting with malli, kanakambara, and the kind of gossip that could derail arranged marriages.

And yet, amidst this beautiful chaos, Raghav's home had remained a stubborn memory.

Of course, the neighbourhood had changed. Two cafés had opened near his street, one of them offering finger millet cookies and Wi-Fi with "ShivaShiva123" as the password. A pharmacy had gone 24/7. The veena teacher had added Google Pay.

This was Malleshwaram — sacred and noisy, floral and caffeinated. A place where Google Calendar reminded you of your yoga class, and your grandmother still reminded you of your raahu kaalam.

And somewhere in between — halfway between benne dosa and the *Bhagavad Gita,* between temple bells and text notifications — lived Raghav. A man who didn't chase trends, but somehow belonged. Soft-spoken in a loud world, timeless in a time that moved too fast.

His father, Srinivasan Shastrigal, was no ordinary priest. He was the priest — the kind whose mere presence made people lower their voices and adjust their panche.

With his broad forehead permanently marked with neatly applied vibhuti lines and a large red kumkum dot, he looked like someone carved out of granite during a full solar eclipse — angular, ageless, and slightly intimidating. His deep-set, unblinking eyes held the stillness of temple oil lamps. His silver-streaked hair was always oiled and combed back tightly, giving him the aura of someone who could summon thunder if a ritual demanded it.

He could recite the Purusha Suktam — that complex Vedic hymn describing the cosmic being — backwards, in his sleep, during a cyclone. It was said that the deity at the temple once nodded in approval mid-homa. Even if that was just Jayalakshmi's exaggeration, Raghav never doubted it.

Raghav grew up steeped in that reverence — no breakfast before *annadana* on weekdays, no morning without mantras. His panche (veshti) folds were sharper than his engineering drawings.

His reflection in the small mirror above the sink surprised him sometimes — not for its vanity, but for its stillness. Dusky skin, warm like first-brewed filter coffee. A trimmed beard that made him look older than his 28 years. Hair thick and wavy, always somewhere between well-combed and mildly chaotic — like it couldn't decide if it was a Sanskrit scholar or a Carnatic drummer.

He wasn't striking in the way films described heroes — no chiseled jawline, no brooding gaze. But there was something else: a quiet gravity. The kind of face that made people lower their voices without realizing. A face that had spent years between temple corridors and physics notebooks, and had never quite learned the art of small talk.

He handled the temple accounts with diligence, balancing donations to the paisa. The temple itself stood like a guardian of time — its gopuram stretching into the sky like a prayer, layered with chiseled deities and stories etched in stone. The granite steps were worn smooth by barefoot feet. As a child, Raghav had traced the carvings on the pillars with his fingers, imagining the gods whispering secrets through stone.

On festival mornings, the temple came alive like a symphony — conch blasts, rustling silk, jasmine-scented devotion, and Raghav moving through it all with a clipboard and the calm of a monk. The sanctum was always lit by a faint oil lamp, flickering against the black granite walls, its silence louder than any conch. The corridors smelled of camphor and turmeric, and Raghav often walked them like a man translating the divine into Excel sheets.

He had also quietly revolutionized the system — introducing digital ledgers, QR code–based donation systems, and real-time festival planning spreadsheets. At first, there had been grumbling. The older trustees raised their eyebrows at "this computer boy's ideas," but soon they began to marvel at how seamlessly the chaos of temple logistics turned into clockwork. Now, even the most orthodox priests asked him to set calendar reminders for muhurtham timings. He oversaw the temple trust's cultural activities — arranging bhajans, finding veena artists for Navaratri, and ensuring the peacock feathers for Krishna skits arrived on time. He was everywhere — at the prasadam counters, backstage during plays, reviewing event budgets on Excel sheets.

Beneath that well-folded cotton and structured order lived a mind like a CERN lab — whirring, burning, questioning.

Because Raghav had a secret love affair. Not with a girl. With science.

By 7 PM, after tallying donations and washing his feet, Raghav would walk to Nagesh's tea stall at the street corner. That's where the transformation happened. His friends — Gopi, a mechanical engineer; Vijay, a freelance graphic designer; and Rahul, an aspiring Kannada rapper — waited for him.

Nagesh's tea shop was where tradition met just enough modernity to stay relevant — and soulful.

Tiled roof, terracotta walls, and a counter lined with copper vessels that caught the afternoon light like molten memory. The shop had proper seating — a few granite-topped tables, wooden-backed chairs rubbed smooth from years of elbows, and a ceiling fan that worked just well enough to stir the scent of tea, cardamom, and rain-washed mud.

At the heart of it all was Nagesh himself — part tea master, part town therapist. His claim to fame was his theatrical tea-pouring style. To mix decoction and milk just right, he'd lift the brass tumbler nearly a meter above the glass and pour in a clean arc of liquid silk. No spillage. No rush. Just confidence earned over thirty years.

"Meter-long tea," Raghav called it — half in jest, half in reverence.

It was chai that hit the soul, not just the throat.

A sleek Bluetooth speaker played a shuffled mix of retro Kannada tracks — Rajkumar ballads, evergreen hits by P. B. Sreenivas, and reimagined *Sugama Sangeetha* remixes. When it rained, the patter on the awning folded into the playlist like ambient percussion.

**Gopi** (stirring tea with a biscuit):

"I'm telling you, da. In five years, AI will replace priests. Just imagine — a bot with eighteen arms doing abhishekam and PayTM-linked prasadam."

**Raghav** (grinning):

"Only if it can chant Rudram in Panini grammar and still stop uncles from cutting ahead in the archana queue."

**Vijay** (mock startup pitch):

"App idea: GodNow™ — Pooja-as-a-Service. Pick deity, select prayer pack, swipe to salvation. Comes with a cloud-based coconut smash animation."

**Rahul** (laughing):

"Version 2.0 — match with a virtual priest who flirts in chaste Sanskrit: 'Kamam me, mano me…' You swipe right for moksha."

**Gopi:**

"Add-on feature: Live Darshan. Choose your angle — drone cam above sanctum or front-facing camera of priest mid-aarti. Premium users get blessings in surround sound."

They laughed.

**Raghav** (quietly):

"You guys joke… but it's possible. Not to replace priests. But to help temples adapt. Imagine a system that manages donations, schedule events, learns local customs — even teaches correct chanting with tone accuracy."

**Vijay** (tilting head):

"You mean… like a Temple Operating System?"

**Raghav** (eyes sharpening):

"Exactly. Most temples run on paper registers and verbal memory. One festival delay, one miscounted annadanam — everything crumbles. I've been digitizing our trust accounts for a year. QR code donations. Automated archana receipts. No one thought it would work. Now they're asking me to integrate horoscope scheduling next."

**Rahul** (half-joking, half-awed):

"Dude… that's kinda brilliant."

**Gopi** (with a mouthful of bajji):

"I thought you were wasting your brain with quantum physics. Turns out, you're making the temple future-proof."

**Vijay** (thoughtful):

"Also… diaspora temples abroad could use this. Where to find a Sanskrit-literate priest at 3 AM in San Jose?"

**Raghav** (softly):

"What if someone in Toronto could book a Grahapravesham with proper muhurtham and live-streamed rituals — with the priest assisted by AI, not replaced by it?"

A gentle silence. Just Ilaiyaraaja's violin solo and the distant sizzle of pakoras on the tava.

**Rahul** (breaking it):

"You might be onto something. This isn't just tech. It's… reverence with reach."

**Gopi** (patting his back):

"Raghav, dai. You're not just Srinivasan Shastrigal's son. You're some kind of… cyber-Agastya."

**Raghav** (smiling faintly):

"I just want to make sure tradition survives without being afraid of tomorrow."

A silence settled—not empty, but full.

The kind of silence people hold when they witness someone standing in their truth.

Gopi, Vijay, Rahul exchanged a look, each of them seeing Raghav in a new light—not just as their friend, but as someone who carried an entire legacy with grace.

Raghav leaned back, eyes sharpening—a man with purpose, unshaken and quietly extraordinary.

**Raghav:** "Did you know Schrödinger and Bohr studied Sanskrit? They didn't think the Upanishads were metaphors. They saw them as quantum principles — just poetically encoded."

He pulled up a PDF on his phone.

**Raghav:**

"Heisenberg once said — 'After the conversations about Indian philosophy, some of the ideas of quantum physics that had seemed so crazy suddenly made much more sense.'"

**Gopi** (grinning):

"Then why can't you talk to a girl, da?"

**Raghav** (without missing a beat):

"Particles are simpler. They follow probabilities. Girls are… wave functions without collapse. You observe them, and they change. You try to measure them, and the parameters shift. Relationships, unlike equations, don't come with constants — just unknowns that refuse to be solved."

**Vijay** (grinning):

"Philosophical, da, but how is that working out for you?"

**Raghav** (smirking faintly):

"For someone like me, used to certainty through calculations, this unpredictability is both awe-inspiring and terrifying. It's like trying to apply quantum theory to rain — you can predict the probability, not when you'll get wet."

**Rahul:**

"Guru! That's your Tinder bio right there."

**Gopi** (laughing hard):

"You'll die a virgin physicist!"

Someone toasted with a Marie biscuit. Another slapped him on the back. Raghav smiled like he always did. But deep inside, the laughter echoed differently.

Because it wasn't a joke to him. He could model black holes, explain the observer effect, and translate Dirac's equations into Sanskrit. But he couldn't decode a smile from across the temple courtyard.

At 10 PM sharp, his mother, Jayalakshmi, would call.

**Jayalakshmi:**

"Raghava, come back. You want Shiva himself to tuck you

in?"

She was the real pillar of the household — managing meals like a schedule, temple gossip like a newsroom, and Raghav's bedtime with loving tyranny. Draped in crisp cotton sarees that rustled like discipline itself, she moved with the energy of someone half her age and the authority of someone twice it. A streak of vibhuti always adorned her forehead, her jasmine flowers never drooped, and her sharp eyes missed nothing — not even a grain of uncooked dal.

Her curd rice could fix almost any emotion. She ruled the kitchen with a ladle and a laser focus — orchestrating her domain with precision. Her rasam had just the right tang, and her Sunday avial could convert non-vegetarians into believers. When she was chopping vegetables, the rhythm could outmatch a mridangam. Once, Raghav tried to sneak a spoonful of payasam before lunch, and she caught him mid-step — without even turning around.

Back home, his father would be seated on the veranda, adjusting his angavastram, sipping hot water.

**Srinivasan:**

"Did you confirm the LED panels for the Navaratri stage?"

**Raghav:**

"Yes, Appa. Also added two extra mics for the bhajan team."

**Jayalakshmi** (placing plate down):

"Eat and sleep. One day, some girl will listen to all this quantum prattle and still ask you what you want for dinner."

**Raghav** (smiling faintly):

"Only if she understands particles and prasad."

His father didn't look up, but smiled.

**Srinivasan:**

"A man who balances bhakti and physics will never be alone."

That night, Raghav folded his panche, placed his phone

on the charging corner, and opened his book of quantum paradoxes. Somewhere in the courtyard, a lone jasmine fell.

And somewhere in the dark, he wondered if there'd ever be someone who could walk between both his worlds — someone who wouldn't see his duality as a contradiction, but as a calling. To be fully seen, not just as the dutiful son in a crisp panche, nor merely the quantum dreamer poring over paradoxes, but as the boy who found symmetry in mantras and particle waves alike. A girl who could sit beside him during Navaratri bhajans and still laugh with him over Heisenberg's uncertainty.

Someone who'd understand why he bowed to the deity, and why he stayed up reading about the universe unraveling at the speed of thought.

## Chapter 3 — The Unmatchable Raghav

At 28, Raghav's life hadn't changed much in years — except for the increasing rate at which his relatives were getting desperate about his bachelorhood. His mother had now started lighting a ghee lamp not just for Lord Vishnu's grace, but for a bride who could cook without garlic. The requirements were evolving.

On most days, Raghav didn't mind being single. He had Schrödinger for mind-bending quantum companionship, Shiva for cosmic stillness and surrender, and a row of perfectly folded white panches (veshti) hanging on his clothesline like disciplined soldiers — sharp, spotless, and awaiting daily duty. His world had symmetry. Silence. Structure.

On certain evenings, especially when his friends laughed over Tinder misadventures or spoke casually of first dates, breakups, and late-night texting, he felt like a forgotten artefact in a cultural museum. Preserved. Pristine. Untouched. As if he were the last surviving specimen of a Brahmin bachelor fluent in both LaTeX and the Lalitha Sahasranamam — a man who could write complex mathematical notations and chant divine verses with equal fluency, but who had never once figured out what to say to a girl who looked him in the eye and smiled.

It wasn't that he lacked confidence. He simply lacked experience. And when algorithms failed to match what mantras couldn't summon, he sometimes wondered: Was there a place in the modern world for someone like him? Someone ancient and algorithmic all at once?

**One more evening at Nagesh's Tea Shop, 7:30 PM**

**Gopi** (wiping samosa oil on his jeans):

"You're telling me you've never kissed a girl?"

**Raghav** (giving a small, crooked smile):

"Once… when I was six. I kissed my neighbor on the cheek during hide and seek. She blushed and ran home."

**Vijay** (leaning forward):

"And then?"

**Raghav:**

"I left a hibiscus near her gate the next morning. Didn't say anything. Just… left it."

**Gopi** (clutching his heart):

"Daawww! Our little temple-Romeo. Six years old and already writing floral poetry."

**Vijay** (laughing):

"You peaked too early, da. That was your golden era!"

Everyone chuckled. Even Raghav. But as the laughter faded and they went back to sipping chai, he stared quietly at the bottom of his glass tumbler. He didn't remember the girl's name. But he remembered how his heart raced. And how good it felt — to be the reason someone smiled and ran.

**Rahul** (joining them at the bench):

"Honestly, though, Raghav… why so much experience in theory, but not in, you know, real-life romance?"

**Raghav** (smirking):

"KG to 12th — Ramakrishna Vidya Mandir. All boys. Teachers are more terrifying than Shiva in Rudra form."

**Gopi:**

"Then college? Surely some hope there?"

**Raghav:**

"Mechanical engineering. Six girls in the whole department."

**Vijay:**

"So you've basically had more equations than conversations."

**Raghav** (mock-defensive):

"Hey, I was on that final-year project team with Anusha… though honestly, I was the only one who did any of the work."

**Rahul** (teasing):

"You didn't just study mechanics. You became one. Fully functional, no emotions."

**Raghav** (grinning):

"Well, I did get emotionally attached to my soldering iron."

**Gopi:**

"Aiyyo. No wonder your mom's doing weekly rituals for your marriage."

They all laughed. The kind of laughter that gently masked the truth.

Still, every now and then, someone in the extended family would decide it was time to take matters into their own hands. A neighbor's niece. A cousin's colleague. A distant Mami's daughter who had a good horoscope and "knew how to make rasam without garlic."

Each proposal arrived with great optimism and even greater WhatsApp forwards.

**So began the occasional — often comical, sometimes confusing — series of matchmaking attempts.**

**Attempt 1: The Crypto Girl**

This match was recommended by a cousin who called the girl a *visionary* —like it was a job title—once in all caps and once with a rocket emoji. It felt less like a marriage proposal and more like a startup pitch.

"She's smart, modern, and works in FinTech. But still wears a saree for pooja," he'd added, as if the saree counterbalanced everything else.

The meeting was set in Shraddha's apartment in Indiranagar.

It was a sleek, air-conditioned museum of modernism—beige walls, designer lamps, and exactly 27 indoor plants, each with a name tag. A brass Nataraja statue near the bookshelf reminded visitors: *We're spiritual but scalable.*

Shraddha's parents welcomed the Shastrigal family at the door with carefully curated warmth. Her father, in a linen kurta and Apple Watch, offered a firm handshake to Srinivasan Shastrigal, while her mother—draped in an elegant handwoven saree—smiled and asked,

"Water? Coconut water? Cold-pressed juice?"

They were gracious, efficient, and well-practiced at hosting—like startup founders meeting angel investors.

Shraddha soon walked out of her room, taking a break from work-from-home duties, and greeted them with a polite warmth that felt slightly rehearsed. She wore a crisp cobalt pantsuit, her shoulder-length hair neatly pinned back, and a tiny maroon bindi—the only softness in an otherwise businesslike appearance. There was grace in her movements, but also the quiet urgency of a calendar reminder ticking in the background.

She served filter coffee in glass tumblers with the efficiency of muscle memory—warm, courteous… and curiously absent.

"Yes, uncle."

"No, aunty, no pets."

"Amma did up the interiors. I just did the lighting plan."

Jayalakshmi Mami was instantly impressed. "Very humble, no? Not at all showy."

Even Raghav found her interesting. Mysterious, even. Like she had an inner Excel sheet constantly updating.

After ten minutes of parental ice-breaking and resume-reading, the adults smiled conspiratorially.

"We'll just leave you two to chat for five minutes," said Shraddha's mother.

They left the room like they were giving toddlers a playdate.

**Shraddha** (slouching back into the sofa):

"Okay, finally. That performance review is over."

**Raghav** (laughing nervously):

"Was it that bad?"

**Shraddha** (shrugging):

"Not bad. Just... templated. Every boy says he's simple, spiritual, and 'open to options.' Are you?"

**Raghav** (blinking):

"I mean... I'm not entirely closed."

**Shraddha** (raising an eyebrow):

"Hmm. I like that. Flexible core values. Adaptable. Market-ready."

There was a brief pause, the kind that sat awkwardly between flattery and formality. Raghav tilted his head slightly, forcing a polite smile while his mind whispered: 'Wait... is she complimenting me, or drafting a LinkedIn endorsement?'

**Shraddha** (as help arrives with snacks):

"So, what food or snack makes you happiest?"

**Raghav** (brightening up instantly):

"Aape payasam."

**Shraddha** (tilting her head):

"Is that a Googleable item?"

**Raghav:**

"No! It's homemade. Rice balls, coconut jaggery, steamed to divinity. Tastes like childhood."

**Shraddha** (grinning):

"That's adorable. Mine's Viel."

**Raghav** (pausing):

"Vile?"

**Shraddha:**

"V-I-E-L. Vegan eel. Lab-grown."

**Raghav:**

"From… seaweed or… the cloud?"

**Shraddha:**

"Startup in Bangalore. They're doing incredible things with protein memory."

Raghav nodded, the way you do when your brain is buffering. Shraddha's tone was brisk but polite, her words clipped like they'd been proofread. He could feel the warmth in her smile, but it didn't quite reach her eyes—they kept flicking toward her laptop in the corner.

Somewhere between "protein" and "memory," he found himself drifting to Appa's advice: 'I should've just married that girl who made rasam.' Rasam didn't require explanation. Rasam didn't need a pitch deck.

**Shraddha** (leaning forward):

"So… what's your day-to-day like? Outside of God and Excel?"

**Raghav:**

"I read… a bit of quantum theory. I'm writing an essay on how Dirac's symmetry might've existed in Shaiva philosophy."

**Shraddha** (freezing mid-sip):

"That's either genius… or spiritual mansplaining."

**Raghav:**

"Hopefully, genius?"

**Shraddha** (laughing):

"You're weird. I like that."

**Raghav** (smiling, genuinely this time):

"Thanks… I think."

**Shraddha:**

"Where do you see yourself in five years?"

**Raghav** (deadpan):

"Hopefully not answering that question in arranged marriage interviews."

They both laugh. The moment softens.

Outside the apartment, Jayalakshmi Mami whispered to Raghav:

**Jayalakshmi** (hushed):

"She talks nicely, but all planned like Google Calendar. No feel."

Raghav just nodded, still trying to process whether Viel was a flavor or a lifestyle.

Match over.

**Attempt 2: The Résumé Bride**

The meeting was set in a modest house in Vidyaranyapura, where plastic sofa covers clung protectively to every cushion, laminated certificates framed past glories on the walls, and the air was dense with the slightly overachieving aroma of agarbatti.

Kavya's parents greeted the Shastrigal family with careful enthusiasm. Her father turned off the television mid-debate and rose with stiff formality, gesturing towards the sofa like a museum guide showing off an exhibit. Her mother, in a neatly pleated cotton saree and gold-rimmed glasses, offered water in stainless steel tumblers and added,

"Please sit… some juice? Or coffee?"

Hovering nearby was Kavya's younger brother — a wiry IT engineer still in his homework hoodie, clearly roped in for logistics like opening the door, moving chairs, pouring water. He nodded politely, then disappeared into a side room, likely to resume a paused call or gaming session.

A moment later, Kavya entered with a tray of juice and a résumé — a literal one. Glossy, two pages, colour-printed. Her salwar-kameez was spotless, her ponytail high and unbending, and her smile exactly calibrated for matrimonial encounters. She looked like someone who colour-coded her ambition and scheduled her emotional bandwidth on Google Calendar.

Jayalakshmi Mami leaned in with the résumé in her hand

and whispered, "Oh, very prepared!"

Raghav murmured back, deadpan, "Should I submit mine too?"

Kavya was polite and pleasant, and her voice had that trained clarity of someone who had once participated in a Toastmasters semi-final.

"I have completed my B.Com, CA Inter, and a data analytics diploma from Coursera," she said, smiling. "I also maintain a food blog and am currently learning German."

Raghav nodded slowly, scanning the résumé. "Wow. That's... a lot."

"I believe in lifelong learning," Kavya said, her voice crisp with conviction. "Do you?"

Raghav hesitated. "Uh… I… recite the Vishnu Sahasranamam every Thursday."

Kavya blinked. Once.

"We'll give you two a few minutes," Kavya's mother said brightly, already ushering the adults toward the kitchen.

Jayalakshmi Mami gave Raghav an encouraging nod — the kind that said *say something intelligent, but also don't mess this up* — before disappearing down the hallway.

Silence settled like plastic sofa covers.

**Kavya:**

"So, what are your short-term goals?"

**Raghav** (thinking):

"Hmm… I'd like to understand the link between dark matter and Shiva's tandava."

**Kavya** (blinks):

"Is that a… real thing?"

**Raghav** (grinning awkwardly):

"The math isn't there yet… but the metaphor is strong."

**Kavya** (blinking again):

"I meant more like—salary, housing, travel bucket list…"

**Raghav:**

"Oh! Right. Uh… I like the mountains. And I'm saving up for a telescope."

Kavya smiled politely — the kind of smile that belongs on a webinar screen.

**Raghav** (trying to recover):

"Your food blog sounds fun. What's it called?"

**Kavya** (brightly):

"@ExcelAndEat. I make dashboards for recipes. Pie charts for pies."

**Raghav** (blinking):

"Wow. Very… metric-based gastronomy."

**Kavya:**

"You have to be precise. Cooking is data."

Another pause. The silence smelled faintly of juice and awkwardness.

Later, on the way back, Jayalakshmi Mami said in the car:

**Jayalakshmi:**

"Nice girl. Sharp mind. Little too sharp. Like blade."

Match archived.

**Attempt 3: Priya**

The third girl, however, was... different.

She was the daughter of Ramanathan, a former student of Srinivasan Shastrigal, someone who still touched his feet with reverence during every temple visit. Her father, Ramanathan, was a soft-spoken civil engineer who still preferred hand-drawn sketches to CAD and measured twice even when the software said it was right the first time. Her mother, Savitha, a retired physics teacher, had that quiet confidence that comes from years of explaining Newton's laws and fixing people's grammar mid-conversation.

They welcomed Raghav's family with warm smiles and

subtle intelligence — sandalwood candles lit in the background; lemon barley water served without fuss.

Their Jayanagar home didn't smell of incense or old filter coffee. It smelled… intentional. Sleek wooden floors, minimalist furniture, and walls that were quietly artistic: a peacock feather painting, a brass bell sculpture, and just one family photo — Priya as a child holding a screwdriver instead of a doll.

She sat by the window in a simple green kurti that complemented her dusky skin, silver jhumkas catching the light with every subtle turn of her head. Her hair was tied in a loose low bun, with a few playful strands escaping — as if even her hairstyle refused to be too serious. Her eyes were kind and quietly curious, the sort that didn't flinch from silence but often found humour tucked within it.

There was a casual elegance to her presence — not the rehearsed poise of someone trying to impress, but the calm confidence of someone who found joy in observing more than performing.

She was a UX designer — someone who believed digital products should behave like well-mannered dinner guests: clear, helpful, and never overstay their welcome.

After polite greetings and a round of lime juice, Srinivasa Shastrigal cleared his throat.

**Srinivasa Shastrigal:** "So, Priya… have you read the Vedas?"

**Priya** (tilting her head playfully): "Does Devdutt Pattnaik's YouTube count?"

He chuckled — visibly caught off guard.

Jayalakshmi Mami, seated beside him, let out a soft but audible, "Aiyyo."

A few minutes later, as tradition demanded, the elders made a discreet exit.

**Jayalakshmi** (murmuring):

"We'll let the kids talk."

The door clicked shut. Silence hovered.

**Priya** (grinning):

"Tell me, are you always this adorably tense, or do I bring out the special edition?"

**Raghav** (trying not to fidget):

"You might be a limited release."

They sat across from each other like two UI wireframes, trying to guess the user flow.

**Raghav:**

"I, uh… I think I've seen you before. At the temple. You sang… *Ganesha Pancharatnam*, right?"

**Priya:**

"Guilty."

**Raghav** (blushing):

"You're the… Ganesha Pancharatnam girl."

**Priya** (laughing):

"That's a new stage name. Should I keep it?"

**Raghav** (smiling):

"It's memorable."

They eased into conversation. She talked about her work — how good design was like good etiquette, invisible but deeply felt. He spoke of symmetry in Shaiva philosophy and how he sometimes compared UX flows to energy systems.

Surprisingly, she followed.

**Priya:**

"Wait — are you saying Vishnu's dashboard is just better designed than Shiva's?"

**Raghav:**

"Exactly. Shiva's interface is divine, but… unpredictable. Like dark mode with thunderbolts."

She laughed — not politely, but with her head tilted back

just slightly, the jhumkas catching the light.

She shared that she once wrote a blog post titled *"Why Astrology Needs a UX Overhaul."* He confessed he was secretly writing a paper on how Dirac's symmetry theory aligned with Nataraja's cosmic dance.

Time blurred.

Eventually, she handed him her phone.

**Priya:**

"Let's not make this a one-time PowerPoint presentation. Number?"

**Raghav** (nodding, fingers trembling):

"Sure..."

He typed his number, accidentally adding an extra zero. She noticed. Deleted. Re-typed. Their thumbs brushed. He froze.

**Priya:**

"Relax. It's not an OTP."

And just like that, she was saved in his phone as **Priya – Pancharatnam Girl.**

Back in the car, on the rain-slick drive home, Raghav stared out of the window. Quiet.

She was warm. Witty. Open.

She didn't mind that he compared the Upanishads to quantum field theory. She even teased him for it.

And she had jhumkas.

But more than anything, she didn't ask him to shrink or simplify.

That tug inside him — it was hope, freshly lit like an oil lamp at dusk.

*Match bookmarked.*

## Chapter 4 — Entangling Hearts

Back home, the glow from the visit to Priya's house hadn't quite faded.

The house was quieter than usual — not heavy quiet, but the kind that follows something promising, like returning from a good concert or discovering the film you almost skipped was actually brilliant.

Raghav changed into his comfort uniform — soft grey shorts and his Einstein T-shirt, where the great man stuck his tongue out, as if mocking everyone else's idea of dignity.

Dinner smelled like reassurance. Amma had conjured dosas, coconut chutney, and a small vessel of sambar still steaming on the stove. Drumsticks bobbed in it like cheerful exclamation marks.

Raghav sat at the dining table, carefully tearing off a piece of dosa and folding it before dipping it into the chutney. Across from him, his father sipped buttermilk, pretending to be buried in *Prajavani* but really circling the subject like a hawk.

Finally, without looking up, he asked:

"So… what do you think of the girl?"

Raghav chewed longer than usual, as if flavor could delay truth.

"She seemed… nice."

"Nice?" Amma raised an eyebrow, sliding another dosa onto his plate. "She welcomed us with lemon barley water and even managed to talk temple architecture with Appa."

"She likes jhumkas and Devdutt Pattanaik," Raghav

murmured, without intending to.

Amma paused. Smiled.

"Aha."

"Grounded girl," Appa said, finally lowering the paper. "Practical. Not flashy. And she actually looked at people when she spoke."

"Unlike the last one," Jayalakshmi Mami chimed in. "That one never looked up from her phone."

"Alright then. I liked her," Amma declared. "She had spark. And she made you look… less like a statue."

Raghav didn't reply. But he dipped the last bit of dosa into both chutney and sambar at once — a daring move for a man who usually kept them separate like rival nations.

It was subtle. But everyone caught it.

That was enough confirmation.

Later, after plates were rinsed and the house slowly wound down for the night, he lay on his bed, legs slightly raised, fingers loosely gripping his phone.

The fan spun above like a hypnotic clock, ticking out loud the fact that he had no idea how to begin a conversation without sounding like an insurance salesman.

He unlocked his phone.

Opened the chat.

Priya — Pancharatnam Girl.

Still there. Still glowing.

He typed:

"Hey:)"

Deleted it. Too enthusiastic. He looked like someone trying to sell dental plans.

Then:

"Nice meeting you today."

Deleted. That wasn't a text — that was a line from an HR orientation video.

Finally:

"Hi Priya."

Neutral. Boring. Impossible to misinterpret.

He hit send before his brain could vote against it.

Fifteen minutes passed. Enough time for him to conclude she'd seen it, thought about it, and decided her life would be better spent joining a Himalayan monastery than replying.

**Priya:**

"Hey there! Took you long enough :P"

**Raghav:**

"Sorry, was just… uh… checking temple events schedule."

He instantly regretted it. Out of all the lies in the world, he'd chosen the most celibate one.

**Priya:**

"Haha, sure. What did you have for dinner?"

**Raghav:**

"Dosas. Amma made them. With sambar and chutney."

He hovered, tempted to delete. Who leads with their mother's menu? But it was too late. Sent.

**Priya:**

"Classic. I ended up with instant noodles."

**Raghav:**

"That still counts as dinner."

**Priya:**

"Barely. But it works when you're too lazy to cook."

He stared at the chat, the corners of his mouth giving away a smile he'd never admit to. It wasn't witty, it wasn't romantic, but it was something. And for him, that already felt like history in the making.

Raghav was cautious — typing, deleting, typing again. Overthinking every word, every pause, every emoji.

Priya was breezy. Effortless. She asked about his Sanskrit classes, his favorite Upanishad, even his weirdest temple mishap.

He told her about the mischievous monkey that once stole his sacred thread during Vishnu Sahasranama.

Priya called it "terrifying and kind of cute." She meant both.

Then—something unexpected.

A new message lit up the screen, soft as a secret:

**Priya:**

"Want to meet tomorrow? Somewhere neutral... Sankey Tank?"

Raghav sat up straighter, heart caught between a stumble and a sprint.

He read it once. Twice. A third time.

Typed: Sure 😊

Paused. Deleted.

Typed it again — slower this time — and hit send.

Silence. Just for a breath.

Then—

**Priya:**

"Cool. Let's say 5 PM tomorrow? I like walking just before sunset."

**Raghav:**

"Sounds perfect."

The message was gone now, floating in digital space, irretrievable.

He leaned back against his pillow, phone glowing in his hand.

The rest of the house had dissolved into its nightly hush — his parents asleep, the temple bell outside gone quiet. Only the ceiling fan hummed, steady as a tabla roll before it finds rhythm.

His T-shirt crinkled against the bedsheet — the same Einstein one, tongue out, mocking the universe — as he turned slightly and looked again at the chat.

This time, he typed deliberately:

**Raghav:**

"Good night, Priya."

The reply came almost instantly:

**Priya:**

"Night, accountant boy :) Don't calculate your heartbeat. Just show up tomorrow."

He smiled. Couldn't help it.

Placed the phone face down, letting its light fade into the dark.

Tomorrow.

Five o'clock.

A walk. With her.

He told himself not to overthink it. But, of course, he already was.

What would he wear? What would he say? Would she notice if he was awkward again? Would it rain?

He closed his eyes.

The fan whirred gently overhead. His heart was still racing, but not in panic — more like anticipation.

And somewhere between all the questions, the excitement, and the hush of Malleshwaram midnight…

Raghav drifted off.

Into the softest, most hopeful sleep he'd had in years.

**The next day.**

A light drizzle misted over Malleswaram's flowering trees, leaving behind a shimmer like the city had been lightly polished overnight. The Gulmohars glowed as if they had bathed in memory.

Raghav rushed through temple duties — archana lists, donation ledgers, and unloading a new crate of bananas for the offering trays. But even through the mantras and the clink of the temple bell, one name looped quietly in his head: Priya.

Across town, Priya shut her laptop after a UI/UX call and drifted into the kitchen. Her mother, in crisp cotton saree tied neatly, stood roasting spices for sambar. She glanced sideways. "Going out?"

Priya poured water from the clay pot, keeping it vague. "Hmm."

"Where to?"

"Sankey Tank."

"Alone?"

Priya smirked. "With Raghav."

There was a pause. Her mother turned from the stove, eyebrows arching.

"The same Raghav who came home last Sunday?"

"Yes," Priya said, lips twitching. "That Raghav. Temple-boy."

Her mother blinked, then stirred slowly. "He seemed… sincere. Nervous. But sincere."

From the living room, her father looked up from his crossword.

"Tell him to walk slowly," he said, pencil tapping.

"Some answers are worth taking time for."

Her mother muttered, "At least he didn't say 'synergy' or call me Ma'am like that other boy."

Priya grinned, grabbing her sling bag. "Relax. It's not a wedding. Just a walk. Maybe coffee."

As she left, her mother called after her:

"Notice his shoes! They say a lot."

In Raghav's quiet Malleswaram home, the late-afternoon light slanted through the grilled window, catching him in front of the mirror.

White polo shirt — ironed, for once — with a faint embroidered collar. His usual jeans, but clean. Hair: somewhere between casually tousled and plainly confused. A dab of vetiver behind his ears. No vibhooti today. Not forgotten—just… this felt like a different kind of darshan.

Jayalakshmi Mami walked in, drying her hands on the edge of her pallu. She eyed him up and down.

"Aiyyo, Raghava. White shirt ironed, hair combed, scent also applied… you're shining like you're going for a job interview!"

Raghav gave a sheepish smile. "Just meeting Priya."

Her eyebrows twitched, but she tried to stay casual.

"Oh, Pancharatnam girl ah? So soon?"

He nodded, smoothing his collar. "She asked if I'd want to meet her at Sankey Tank."

Jayalakshmi circled him like an appraiser. "Jeans is familiar. The shirt is ambitious. Hair is… undecided. Perfume is trying too hard to be casual."

Raghav laughed. "Anything else, Ma?"

She leaned in, mock-conspiratorial. "Don't bring up particle physics. Or temple donation analytics. Compliment her looks. Walk straight. Speak clearly."

He slipped on his sandals, halfway out already.

**Sankey Tank — 4:50 PM**

It was slightly cloudy, which only added to the charm. Sankey Tank — a nineteenth-century man-made lake tucked between Malleshwaram and Sadashivanagar — had the polite hush of a place that refused to shout. The city's noise seemed to dissolve at its edges; along the path, walkers, couples, and students with headphones kept an unhurried rhythm.

Raghav arrived ten minutes early and picked a bench facing the water — a small, breathing rectangle of calm. Ripples drifted toward the far bank, past the outline of a tree-shaded island where cormorants and other water birds kept sentinel.

He kept his phone in his hand — unlocking it, relocking

it — nervous energy made him fidget.

He even turned to Google: **"conversation starters for a first date"** — then closed it in embarrassment.

He whispered to himself: "Don't be a mess… just be yourself… whatever that is."

He saw her first — Priya, casually striding toward him in jeans, a black top, silver jhumkas glinting in the fading sunlight, a canvas tote slung over her shoulder.

She smiled warmly — a simple, disarming expression — and walked up.

**Priya:**

"Hey. Did you come straight from adding up your account books?"

**Raghav:**

"Actually… I might have finished them a bit faster today. Just for… this."

**Priya:**

"Aww."

They fell into step, side by side — close, but not touching — a little nervous, a little unsure, yet comfortable.

He kept wondering: Should I say something clever? Should I break the silence?

**Priya:**

"Has your mom asked for a horoscope match yet?"

**Raghav:**

"She tried, but our priest said Mercury was in retrograde."

**Priya:**

"Did you tell him it always is?"

**Raghav:**

"I did. He raised his voice."

**Priya** (laughs):

"Oh man… your family. So dramatic."

They paused near a large rain tree. A bushy-tailed squirrel

darted past. Priya turned toward a nearby bench.

**Priya:**

"Want to sit?"

They sat on the stone bench, the lake spread out in front of them like a calm secret.

**Raghav:**

"You know… Sankey Tank isn't just for evening walks. It was built in the 1880s by Colonel Richard Sankey, an engineer, when Bangalore was running out of water. Basically — Victorian-era crisis management."

**Priya** (grinning):

"Only you would start a first-date story with 'Victorian-era crisis management.'"

**Raghav** (half-embarrassed, half-proud):

"What can I say? Romance looks different in my head."

**Priya:**

"Go on. Now I want the full 'Bangalore Water Board: Love Story Edition.'"

**Raghav** (laughs):

"Well… my grandfather used to bring me here as a kid. He'd say the whole city owed this lake its thirst-quenching. I didn't really get it then — I just liked watching the cormorants, and throwing puffed rice into the water. Once, a fish actually jumped high enough to splash me. I thought it was saying thank you."

**Priya** (softly):

"That's… sweet."

**Raghav:**

"Or deeply nerdy. Depends on who's listening."

**Priya** (teasing, but warm):

"Lucky for you, I happen to find 'nerdy civil engineering bedtime stories' ridiculously attractive."

**Raghav** (laughs):

"See, that's what I mean. This place was... magical. A whole little world for kids. Now it's just joggers with earphones and college students on their third date."

**Priya:**

"Don't forget middle-aged uncles discussing real estate prices."

**Raghav** (smiling):

"True. It feels like the lake has grown up, gotten serious."

**Priya** (tilts her head at him):

"Which is exactly what you're trying not to do."

He laughed, a little shy, but didn't disagree. The water caught the lights from the promenade, scattering them into restless constellations, as if the lake itself still remembered how to play.

**Raghav:**

"See the lights along the path?"

**Priya:**

"Mm-hm."

**Raghav:**

"They... in the water, they look like—"

**Priya:**

"Like what?"

**Raghav:**

"Like that Van Gogh painting. The swirly one."

**Priya:**

"Starry Night?"

**Raghav:**

"Yeah. But here, the stars are just street lamps. And the swirls are ripples."

**Priya:**

"Still beautiful."

The air had turned gentle, holding them both. The reflected lights danced on the ripples, as if the lake had decided to flirt with the night. Somewhere, a duck made a low, contented sound.

Priya smiled to herself, thinking: Maybe this evening is painting itself into something beautiful.

**Priya:**

"Actually… there's a really nice Italian restaurant nearby — Little Italy. Want to try?"

**Raghav:**

"Sounds perfect."

They turned down a small lane from Sankey Tank. The restaurant's entrance was marked by a wrought-iron gate and a vine-covered arch. Inside, Little Italy glowed with a soft, amber warmth — small lamps on the tables, fairy lights strung across wooden beams. The furniture was a blend of rustic and elegant, with heavy wooden tables and comfortable benches. The air was rich with basil, tomato, and freshly-baked bread.

The maître d' nodded in recognition and led them to a corner table by a large window, offering a view of a small garden shimmering under the sunset's glow.

Raghav held the back of Priya's seat as she sat — a nervous but sincere gesture — then slipped into his own seat across from her. The moment seemed to hang in time — a mixture of nervousness, growing affection, and the quiet thrill that something new was just beginning.

Just then, the waiter approached — warm smile, leather-bound menu in hand.

**Waiter:**

"Are you ready to order, or would you like a minute?"

Priya gave Raghav a teasing glance before answering.

**Priya:**

"We're ready."

She ordered her risotto — mushrooms, extra parmesan.

Raghav followed, each syllable pronounced like careful

code.

"The… um… gnocchi pomodoro, please."

The waiter nodded and swept away the menus.

Priya leaned in, eyes dancing.

**Priya:**

"Did I drag you somewhere you're not comfortable?"

**Raghav:**

"Not at all. I love Italian food. I just… panic with menus. Too many vowels."

Priya laughed softly.

**Priya:**

"So you needed a risk analysis before ordering gnocchi?"

**Raghav:**

"Exactly. And still… I was 70% sure I'd regret not copying your order."

Right then, the waiter returned with their plates — her risotto steaming, his gnocchi glowing in pomodoro sauce.

**Raghav** (tasting, then nodding):

"Okay, this is good. Life-changing good."

**Priya:**

"See? Not a disaster."

**Raghav:**

"Food is never neutral, Priya. Choose badly, and the whole evening is rewritten."

**Priya** (teasing):

"Dramatic. Next, you'll say pasta shapes determine destiny."

**Raghav** (serious now, leaning in a little):

"Maybe not pasta… but connection, yes."

He hesitated, then leaned in a little more.

**Raghav:**

"You know about quantum entanglement?"

**Priya** (smiling):

"I should've guessed physics was hiding under the gnocchi.

Go on."

**Raghav:**

"Two particles — born from the same source — remain connected, no matter the distance. Touch one, and the other feels it instantly. They're not just near each other, they belong to the same hidden pattern."

**Priya** (softer now):

"And in your head, that's like… people?"

**Raghav:**

"Yes. Like two lives entangled. Even if chaos surrounds them, there's this thread — unseen, but unbreakable. It's not randomness. It's… fate, disguised as physics."

For a moment, she just looked at him, her spoon idle.

**Priya** (half-smiling):

"You really are impossible. Who else compares love to particle physics over gnocchi?"

**Raghav** (nervous laugh):

"Sorry, I overdo these things."

**Priya** (interrupts, warm):

"Don't be sorry. That's why it works. You make the world less ordinary."

This time again, Raghav fell silent — unsure how to respond — then turned his face toward the water.

They then walked slowly back; now the sky was a deep velvet, and the path lamps glowed like quiet promises.

Raghav's pulse was a wild mess — but he kept up, matching her stride. Side by side, their footsteps fell into rhythm — quiet, careful, almost musical.

As they rounded the final curve near the lake, Priya casually let her hand drift closer to his — just a soft, unconscious move. A moment. A spark.

Raghav noticed. Froze.

His hand stayed close, too close — unsure whether to

move toward hers or away. His heart wanted to reach out, to hold that warmth. But his nerves held him back. The weight of hesitation — fear, inexperience, maybe both — tugged at him.

Priya noticed. She didn't pull away.

Instead, she reached again — gently — her fingers brushing against his.

This time, he felt it like a jolt. He froze again, caught in that delicate space between instinct and uncertainty.

She didn't flinch. Didn't tease. Just smiled softly and said:

**Priya** (whispering):

"It's okay. I know. We're figuring this out together."

He nodded — not with words, but with something deeper. A nervous mess. A happy mess. A mess blooming just the way he was meant to.

She booked an Ola cab, and within minutes, the headlights washed over the curb. As she walked toward the waiting cab, he watched — not with longing, but with a quiet, glowing hope. The kind that whispered something real had just begun.

She gave him a smile that felt like it might last in his memory longer than the evening.

He waited until the cab turned the corner, then walked to the parking lot where his Ather stood under a lone streetlight. The electric hum was soft, almost conspiratorial, as he glided out onto the quiet streets. The cool wind pressed against his face, carrying the scent of rain-soaked leaves.

Happiness pulsed in him — the kind that made the city lights look softer, friendlier. And yet, beneath it, a tiny ache lingered: he'd walked beside her for hours, but never quite found the courage to take her hand.

Somewhere between Sanky tank and home, he laughed at himself. Maybe next time.

His phone buzzed just as he reached home. It was Priya's message.

**Priya:**
"Still nervous?"
He typed.
Deleted.
Typed again.
Paused.
**Raghav:**
"Less than before.
But still praying Mercury behaves."
A moment later, her reply popped up:
**Priya:**
"Mercury can behave… but I wasn't planning to."
He stared at it, a half-grin spreading, half-panic returning.
It was bold, mischievous, utterly her.

And it left him feeling like maybe chaos wasn't something to fear at all.

## Chapter 5 — The Arrival of FlirtBuddy

That night, Raghav lay flat on his back, staring up at the ceiling fan as it spun in slow, repetitive circles — a mechanical echo of his mind.

He hadn't meant to pull away when Priya briefly touched his hand. He hadn't meant to ruin the moment.

But he did.
And now, regret.

He sighed, picked up his phone, and typed:
"How to stop overthinking with women?"
"How to not freeze when someone likes you?"
"Best AI dating coach?"

Click. Scroll. Swipe. Click again.

And then, like a little miracle—or maybe just a cosmic joke with impeccable timing—there it was.

**FlirtBuddy — your digital wingman with emotional intelligence.**

The app. Glowing on his screen like it had been waiting for this exact moment, for him, specifically, after all his fumbling and fretting:

Raghav stared at it, heart fluttering with something between hope and terror. It was ridiculous. It was absurd. And yet...

somehow, in that tiny, neon glow, it felt like destiny. Divine, even.

Behind FlirtBuddy is Bae-ngaluru Works, far from your typical tech startup. These part-time cupids and full-time troublemakers have sharpened their skills amidst Koramangala's buzzing coffee shops and Bengaluru's ever-evolving dating scene. With a blend of behavioral psychologists, savvy AI engineers, and hopeless romantics, they set out to create more than just another dating app.

Their creation? A cheeky, emotionally intelligent wingman designed to spark conversations, dodge those dreaded awkward silences, and maybe even throw in a playful roast. From their open-plan office — packed with beanbags, patchy Friday Wi-Fi, and a whiteboard full of terrible pick-up lines — this team is coding a flirtation revolution that's witty, charming, and totally irresistible.

The app store reviews were strange — and glowing:

- "Made me believe in romance again."
- "Kind, cheeky, and surprisingly accurate."
- "Like having a therapist, meme page, and Karan Johar whisperer in your pocket."

Raghav hit download.

FlirtBuddy didn't descend with thunder or a blinding ray of light.

It arrived like a shimmering notification. A pixelated wink. A soft rush of color across his screen.

A riotous deity made of code, psychology, and mischievous charm.

An animated welcome video played — minimalist, elegant, like a new MacBook onboarding screen:

**Welcome to FlirtBuddy.**

Your digital wingman.

Your emotional translator.

Your chaos-optimized co-pilot for modern love.

A sleek, vibrant logo appeared — a glowing heart wearing headphones, winking mid-swish — somewhere between a DJ, a therapist, and a friend who sends voice notes at 2 a.m.

Then came the voice.

Confident. Warm. A little sarcastic. Like your cousin who knows how to talk to anyone at weddings but also reads Jung for fun.

*"Hey there, fresh heart. I'm FlirtBuddy."*

*"I'm the bridge between your overthinking brain and your underused flirting muscle."*

*"Think of me as your co-pilot on the rollercoaster of attraction — trained on:*

🧠 *Behavioral psychology*

💬 *Conversation timing*

❤️ *Attachment theory*

🤖 *3,42,000 failed first dates (don't ask)*

🎭 *Meme culture and Karan Johar films*

*...so you don't have to overthink your way through love."*

The colors shifted subtly, calming — like dusk turning into evening.

*"I won't ghost you. I won't judge you. I won't send you cringey pick-up lines."*

*"Unless you ask nicely."*

*"You bring the sincerity. I'll bring the sparkle."*

*"Together, we'll turn your love life from overthought WhatsApp drafts to spontaneous tabla jam sessions."*

*"So, shall we begin?"*

A button blinked at the bottom of the screen:

**[Let's Go 💖]**

Raghav hesitated. Then tapped.

A small pulse of color flowed across the screen, like something sacred had just begun.

FlirtBuddy presented a short intake form — a mix of quirky questions meant to gauge his romantic profile:

*"Alright, mystery human... before I start coaching you into your Karan-Johar-level romance arc, I need to know you better."*

*"No lengthy forms. No judgment. Just a vibe check. Ready?"*

Raghav nodded instinctively, though no one was watching

**🌟 Romantic Profile Setup — FlirtBuddy Style**

A bright, bubbly screen appeared with quirky questions and soft animations dancing in the margins — teacups clinking, hearts bouncing, a violin emoji stretching.

FlirtBuddy's voice guided him through:

" 🍿 ***Q1: Who is the fictional couple you secretly root for?"***

**Raghav** (typing, cautiously):

"Virat and Anushka in real life.

And maybe... Ranbir and Alia in *Brahmāstra*. There's something about the way they trust each other. It feels... grounded."

**FlirtBuddy:**

*"Got it. You're looking for real chemistry with cosmic undertones. Intimacy + warmth + a side of slow burn = noted.*

*Sternberg's Love Triangle agrees. You're an intimacy-passion-commitment kind of guy."*

" 🎬 Q2: ***Who's your cinematic wingman style?"***

**Raghav** (nervously):

"Shah Rukh Khan, when he's being vulnerable.

That scene in Kal Ho Naa Ho, where he confesses without expecting anything back..."

**FlirtBuddy:**

*"Oof. Soft boy alert. Sincere. Old-school. You're not here to*

*impress — you're here to connect. You're made for love letters, not dating apps. Classic."*

"🧠 ***Q3: What do you overthink the most before texting someone you like?"***

**Raghav** (sighs, typing slowly):

"Everything.

Is this too formal?

Too needy?

Too many emojis?

Will she think I'm boring?"

**FlirtBuddy:**

*"Classic Text Paralysis Syndrome. Don't worry, I come with a built-in Overthink Neutralizer."*

Also known as perspective."

" ☕ ***Q4: What feels more like 'you'?***

*a) Sunset rooftop, soft jazz, warm silences*

*b) Beachside café, chaotic laughter, weird dance moves*

*c) Temple corridor, shared glances, quiet understanding*

*d) Rainy bookstore, two mugs of chai, a shared blanket of words."*

**Raghav** (selects d):

"That last one… the rainy bookstore."

**FlirtBuddy** (grinning):

*"Aha! You're a deep-souled chai-lover with a poetic core. Got it. I'll program your flirt style accordingly — less 'pick-up lines,' more 'poetic timing"*

💾 **FlirtBuddy Configuration: COMPLETE**

*The screen buzzed softly. A loading bar filled with tiny hearts.*

**FlirtBuddy:**

*"Alright, buddy. Configuration complete. I know just enough about your heart to not mess it up (yet).*

*You're a soft-spoken romantic with sincere eyes and a dangerously high emoji-deletion rate.*

*I'm going to be your wingman, your therapist, your hype squad, and, if needed, your emoji intervention hotline."*

Raghav stared at the ceiling — the same quiet heaviness returning, mixing with hope, confusion, and something warm he couldn't name.

**Raghav** (softly):

"Buddy… can I ask you something before I sleep?"

**FlirtBuddy** blinked awake again.

*"Oh? A late-night confession? Proceed, starboy. My circuits are listening."*

**Raghav** exhaled — slow, shaky.

"Something happened yesterday. With Priya."

**FlirtBuddy's** avatar sat up straighter, hands steepled like a discount therapist.

*"Now we're talking. Begin narrative download."*

**Raghav** hesitated — then added quietly:

"Actually… I should start a little earlier.

Priya is— well, she's someone I met… as a marriage alliance."

**FlirtBuddy** froze mid-animation.

*"Plot twist detected. Proceed."*

**Raghav** continued:

"Our families matched our horoscopes, set up a meeting, the usual awkward tea and biscuits routine."

He paused, remembering.

"But with her… it wasn't awkward. She laughed easily. She listened. She asked real questions — not resume questions."

"She said she liked my 'nerdy charm.' I'm still not sure if she meant it or was being polite."

A faint smile.

"But I felt… seen. Maybe for the first time."

He swallowed.

"We met again — just the two of us. A walk around Sankey Tank, then dinner.
She made me talk more than I usually do. I don't know how she did that."

**FlirtBuddy:**

*"Ah, classic. The Rare Human Who Knows How To Disarm A Shy Heart."*

**Raghav** nodded, eyes softening at the memory:

"Everything felt easy with her. Natural.

Like I didn't have to pretend to be… anything else."

He took a breath — then continued.

"After dinner, we were walking by the lake. Talking… laughing. Everything felt easy.

And then… she reached for my hand."

His voice caught.

**FlirtBuddy:**

*"Ah. The Hand-Holding Threshold. Go on."*

**Raghav** (whispered):

"I froze,".

"Not a small freeze. A full… system shutdown.

I wanted to hold her hand — really wanted to — but I couldn't move."

**FlirtBuddy** nodded dramatically.

*"Continue. Symptoms consistent so far."*

**Raghav** (whispered):

"She tried again. Gently. Twice.

And both times… I froze."

He swallowed.

"She didn't tease. She didn't get upset. She just whispered, 'It's okay. We're figuring this out together.'"

FlirtBuddy paused — the glow around its avatar softening.

**Raghav:**

"Buddy… what's wrong with me? Why can't I just do the simplest thing when I actually like someone?"

**FlirtBuddy** leaned in, voice warm but firm:

*"Listen carefully, Raghav.*

*You're not malfunctioning. You're overwhelmed."*

*"You freeze because the moment feels real.*

*Because it matters — too much.*

*Your heart leaps… and your body pulls the handbrake."*

Raghav blinked, like someone finally being seen.

**FlirtBuddy** lowered its tone.

*"Trust me — I've seen worse.*

*I once had a client who said 'Love you' to a cab driver.*

*Another one panicked during a hug and dropped his phone inside a fountain."*

Raghav's lips twitched despite himself.

**FlirtBuddy:**

*"You? You're a slow-bloom romantic with sincere circuitry.*

*Your feelings arrive instantly.*

*Your actions arrive later.*

*Like a delayed train, but still heading the right way."*

A tiny animation appeared — two pixelated hands inching closer, not touching yet, just… trying.

**FlirtBuddy:**

*"And Priya? She didn't walk away.*

*She saw your heart glitch… and reached again.*

*That's not a red flag.*

*That's the universe sending you a software update."*

Raghav let out a breath he didn't know he'd been holding.

**FlirtBuddy** winked.

*"For the next time, I'll coach you. We are doing this consciously and courageously."*

A small, shy smile warmed Raghav's face. His heart was beating faster than usual — not with fear, but with a feeling he hadn't known in a long time: hope.

**Raghav** (yawning):

"Okay, Buddy… I think I need to… sleep."

**FlirtBuddy** (in a hush-toned display):

*"Sleep well, starboy. Your love life isn't going anywhere — except upward. Dreams are just subconscious simulations anyway."*

Raghav smiled, closed his phone, and pulled the sheet over his chest. For the first time in weeks, his mind didn't wander into overthinking or ritual to-do lists. It simply rested. A small, happy mess drifting into sleep.

**Next Morning: The Real-World Beckons**

The morning temple bells chimed through the soft golden light. Fresh tulsi leaves glistened with dew, and sandalwood smoke danced in the air as the first rituals began.

**Raghav,** draped in his panche (veshti), moved through his duties with practiced ease — sorting the temple accounts, organizing the donation receipts, refilling the brass lamps. His hands were steady, but his mind… was elsewhere.

All day, **Raghav** felt the hum of excitement beneath his calm surface. His thoughts kept drifting back to the shimmering arrival, the warm voice that said things like "Your love life just got an upgrade" and "Dreams are just subconscious simulations."

By late afternoon, as he handed a receipt to a visiting devotee and double-checked the flower vendor's bill, he found himself checking the clock more than once.

For once, it wasn't the daily prayer timings he was looking at. It was time itself — ticking toward that one quiet hour where he could sit alone… and log back in.

**🏙 Evening: Return of the Digital Deity 🏙**

**Raghav** reached home just before sunset. He changed

into a soft cotton tee, poured himself a tumbler of rose milk, and settled on the edge of his bed like a boy about to unwrap something secret.

He opened his phone.

The screen lit up like a warm hug.

**FlirtBuddy** (playfully):

*"Welcome back, oh seeker of awkward romance and hidden potential. Ready for Simulation Mode?"* 🎥 ✨

**Raghav** (typing, grinning):

"Kind of. Yes. Maybe. Let's try?"

**FlirtBuddy:**

*"That's the spirit. This isn't school. It's a rehearsal for your own movie.*

*I'm your script doctor, romantic stunt double, and backstage cheerleader.*

*Let's begin…"*

As the screen pulsed with soft amber hues, **FlirtBuddy** appeared again — shimmering slightly, as if its presence had been recharged with cosmic caffeine.

**FlirtBuddy** (gently teasing):

*"Before we dive into simulated awkward eye contact and imaginary cappuccinos, let's get something straight, my dear human-in-progress."*

**Raghav** (laughing nervously):

"Okay…"

**FlirtBuddy:**

*"I'm not just some cheeky chatbot trying to teach you cheesy pick-up lines.*

*I'm a learning interface — part emotional mirror, part romantic sparring partner, and part algorithm trained on thousands of real, complicated, beautiful human interactions."*

**Raghav** sat a little straighter.

**FlirtBuddy** (warmly, like a friend leaning closer):

*"I'm built to help you practice.*

*To guide you through the jitters.*

*To offer simulations that don't judge, but teach — through playful trial and delightful error.*

*No likes, no swipes, no performance anxiety.*

*Just you, slowly becoming more… you."*

A pause. Then the screen glowed softly.

**FlirtBuddy:**

*"My mission?*

*Not to make you someone else.*

*But to help you show up as your best self — the version that doesn't freeze when someone touches your hand, the version that knows what he wants and how to say it — with clarity, honesty, and a touch of charm."*

**Raghav** smiled faintly, both comforted and curious.

**FlirtBuddy** (playfully):

*"And look — I get it.*

*Love is terrifying.*

*It's like trying to do a physics exam while riding a rollercoaster blindfolded —*

*But with fewer equations and more feelings.*

*But here's the trick: you don't have to be perfect.*

*You just have to show up."*

**Raghav:**

"So… how does this work exactly?"

**FlirtBuddy** (suddenly professional — like a very handsome PowerPoint):

*"Here's what I've got for you:*

◇ **Simulated Conversations**

• *You'll talk to virtual characters I generate — charming, quirky, sometimes confusing — just like real people.*

• *You'll practice breaking the ice, sharing emotions, and responding to tricky moments.*

• *Think of it like rehearsal for the real stage.*

◇ **Emotional Feedback & Tips**

• *After each simulation, I'll gently highlight what worked, what didn't, and how you can grow.*

• *I'll quote real relationship psychology too — but never in a boring way, promise.*

◇ **Customization**

• *As we go, I learn from you.*
*Your style. Your fears. Your humor. Your hopes.*
*And I tailor your training accordingly.*

◇ **Zero Judgment. Full Growth.**

• *This is your space. Private, kind, and completely yours."*

**FlirtBuddy** *(softer now):*

*"You've already done the bravest thing:*
*You admitted you want help.*
*Now...*
*Shall we begin?"*

**Raghav** took a deep breath, held the phone like it was a little magic wand, and nodded.

◇ **Simulation 1 — Breaking the Ice** ◇

*Powered by FlirtBuddy: Your Personal Wingman in the Cloud*

The screen on Raghav's phone shimmered softly, then expanded into full-screen mode — golden light washing over digital velvet curtains as if a grand romantic opera was about to begin.

A friendly chime rang out — not aggressive, not robotic — more like a soft marimba that made the nervous heart feel welcome.

**FlirtBuddy** (voice smooth, mischievous):

*"Alright, superstar, welcome to your very first Simulation Arena™.*

*Where awkward silences are allowed, flubs are fine, and every 'umm…' is a step toward greatness."*

**Raghav** adjusted his pillow behind him and blinked. The screen changed…

🖼 **Visual Environment: A Café in Indiranagar**

The screen now resembled a beautifully lit café — all deep leather tones and sunlight filtering through French windows. Smooth jazz floated through the scene, the kind that made you want to lean forward instead of scroll away.

Vintage bulbs hung low over polished wooden tables. A bookshelf wrapped around the back wall, half-stuffed with forgotten paperbacks and ceramic elephants. Waiters moved slowly. Nobody was in a rush.

**Raghav** felt himself sitting — or rather, his avatar — at a corner table with two steaming cups of coffee.

Just as he was admiring the detailing in the latte foam, a voice spoke beside him.

🗨 **Simulated Character: Simran**

**Simran** was charming, confident, and warm. Not intimidating, just… present. She looked **Raghav** in the eye and smiled with a little tilt of the head.

**Simran:**

*"Hey… is this seat taken?"*

**Raghav** (nervously typing into the interface):

"Ah… I… I think… It's not. Please… sit. I'd be delighted."

**Simran** *chuckled, slid into the seat, and gave him a kind look.*

**Simran:**

*"You know, nervous guys are kind of my favorite. Especially the ones who say 'I'd be delighted' like it's a Jane Austen novel."*

**FlirtBuddy** (whispering on the side):

*"Note: humor is working. Confidence is not required; honesty is enough. Proceed, Romeo."*

A prompt popped up: **Pay a sincere compliment.**

**Simran** (teasing, leaning forward):

*"Alright, mysterious stranger. Compliment me — something real. Not the 'nice smile' stuff. Something you noticed."*

**Raghav** (pausing, then typing slowly):

"Your book. You're reading *The Great Gatsby.*

I always felt… it was a tragedy disguised as a love story.

That feeling of loving someone deeply… but never quite getting there.

It's sad. But beautiful."

**Simran** looked down at her book, then back at him, surprised.

**Simran** (softly):

*"That's… actually kind of perfect. Most people just comment on the cover. I think you're deeper than you let on."*

🧠 **FlirtBuddy Debrief**

The screen froze with a soft shimmer. **FlirtBuddy's** face appeared with confetti in the background, as if **Raghav** had just passed Level 1 in a game of kindness.

**FlirtBuddy:**

" 🎉 **Simulation Complete — Breaking the Ice: Level 1** 🎉

💡 **Key Wins:**

✅ *Sincere compliment — not superficial*
✅ *Embraced nervousness without apology*
✅ *Allowed a real thought to lead the way*
✅ *Created emotional resonance, not just banter*

🧠 **Insight (from Psychology Research):**

*Compliments that reference personal observations — like what someone's reading — signal that you see them. This builds trust (Gottman, 1999).*

🎯 **Tip:**

*Don't rush to impress. Be curious. Curiosity is the most underrated form of flirtation."*

The café dimmed, and the screen returned to its warm home screen.

**FlirtBuddy** (cheering quietly):

*"One down, buddy. You're doing better than you think.*

*Shall we take it up a notch?"*

### ◇ Simulation 2 — Turning Up the Charm ◇

*Powered by FlirtBuddy's Confidence Algorithm™ (Now with 32% more Swag)*

The screen on **Raghav's** phone flickered to life again. This time, the marimba chime was layered with a soft tabla beat, hinting at mischief and melody.

A title card appeared like the opening shot of a film:

"Scene 2: Rooftop Café. Evening.

There's a breeze in the air and hope in your chest.

And guess what — you're not nervous. You're romantic."

**FlirtBuddy** (voice slightly lower, charming):

*"Okay, Romeo 2.0 — this one's cinematic. This is your rainy rooftop moment. You're not just surviving conversation — you're sparking connection. Breathe in. Let go of 'trying to be good.' Just… be real."*

🖼 **Visual Environment: Rooftop Café in Indiranagar**

The digital scene now morphed into a breezy rooftop — glowing fairy lights draped overhead; rustic tables lit with lanterns. The skyline of Bangalore shimmered in the background, streaked with gold and pink. Soft indie music played — something with longing in the chords.

People were laughing gently, clinking cups. There was a romantic hush in the air, like the city was waiting for someone to say something honest.

**Simran 2.0** returned — this time, in a soft cotton kurta, her hair pulled back casually, like she'd just stepped out of a Gautham Menon film.

**Simran:**

*"Hey… I think I know you from somewhere…"*

**Raghav** (slow smile forming, still a little unsure):

"Maybe… I come here often… or I wish I did.

I'm more of a stay-in-and-listen-to-rain kind of person."

**Simran** (giggling):

*"Same. Big fan of rain and long silences.*

*So, tell me… are you a silent guy or a music guy?"*

**Raghav** (warming up):

"Bit of both, I think. I love old Hindi lyrics.

Also… I'm a Karan Johar fan. Especially the rain scenes.

They feel like… poetry with thunder."

**Simran** (softening):

*"God, same.*

*You know the Kuch Kuch Hota Hai one? Rahul and Anjali in the rain?*

*I cry. Every. Single. Time."*

**Raghav** (smiling deeper now):

"Yeah. That moment… it feels like something you can't fake.

Raw, stupid, beautiful.

I think I'd want love like that — a little messy, but fully felt."

**Simran** was quiet for a second — in a good way. She looked out at the clouds.

**Simran** (softly):

*"That's rare, you know.*

*Most people pretend to be cool. You're… just real."*

**Raghav** reached for his mocktail and took a sip, calming his nerves. Then, feeling brave:

**Raghav:**

"Would you want to… grab a coffee again sometime? Maybe without the simulated background music?"

**Simran** (soft smile):

*"Yeah… I'd like that."*

She handed him her phone, and he typed his name in — resisting the urge to add a little smiley. When she took it back, their fingers brushed, light as a breath, before she slipped it into her bag.

🧠 **FlirtBuddy Debrief (With Fireworks)**

**FlirtBuddy** (jumping in with sparkles and virtual roses):

🔥 **Simulation 2 Complete — Turning Up the Charm** 🔥

" 💡 **Key Wins:**

✅ *Honest over clever*

✅ *Used cultural reference to spark shared emotion*

✅ *Created intimacy without needing to push*

✅ *Took a risk — made a real ask*

🧠 **Insight (Social Psychology Tip):**

*When two people experience mutual nostalgia or shared emotional references, they feel like they've 'known each other forever' (Collins & Miller, 1994). Rain scenes, old songs, and childhood memories are emotional shortcuts.*

🎯 **Pro Move:**

*Don't try to 'close the deal', just open a door — softly, sincerely. And let the other person walk through."*

The rooftop faded, and **Raghav's** real-world room blinked back into view. His phone screen shimmered with gentle praise.

**FlirtBuddy** (voice warm, almost human):

*"You did it, buddy. You danced with the moment.*

*That's what charm is — not being perfect, but being present."*

**FlirtBuddy** (appears back in coach mode, leaning on a virtual console, grinning):

*"Okay, my charming chaos theory enthusiast… pause the jazz music, because we need to talk.*

*You just wrapped Simulation 2 like a natural. Nervous? Yes. But real? Absolutely. That's the sweet spot."*

*A progress bar appears: 62% Confidence Unlocked. One pixelized heart fills in.*

**FlirtBuddy** (softer now):

*"But here's the thing, Raghav…*

*No simulation can ever recreate the tiny tremble in your thumb before you hit send.*

*Or the sound of your own heart when a real person texts back.*

*What did we just do?*

*That was the warm-up band.*

*Now it's time for the main act — Reality."*

The interface gently fades. A simpler screen appears: *Message Priya?*

**FlirtBuddy** (warmly, one last nudge):

*"Go on. Carry your nervous grace, your soft science, and your silly hopes into the real world.*

*And hey — no matter what happens, I'm here. Right in your pocket.*

*Ready to cheer when you fly… or hold your hand when you trip."*

Beat. Then with a wink:

*"Now go text the girl. I'll queue up the happy playlist."*

**◇ The Real-Life Challenge: Priya ◇**

**Status: LIVE | Environment: Your Actual Life | Stakes: Your Actual Heart**

Raghav sat still in his room — phone in hand, heart skipping like a scratched record. The simulations had warmed him up, but this? This was Priya. The girl who made his pulse trip and his language double-check itself.

And this time, there was no rewind button.

His phone buzzed gently — a reminder from FlirtBuddy:

**FlirtBuddy:**

*"This is it, Superstar.*

*This isn't a rooftop café built from pixels.*

*This is your story now.*

*Write it with your heart — and don't worry, I'm still here."*

Raghav smiled, nervous again — but a little less frozen. He stood up, walked towards his window, looked out at the quiet Bangalore skyline, and began typing.

📝 Message Attempt 1:

"Hey, I was thinking…"

He paused. Backspaced.

Attempt 2:

"Had fun last time. Want to meet again?"

Too bland. Delete.

Attempt 3:

He let out a long breath. Closed his eyes. Typed with the clarity that comes only when you stop pretending.

"Hey Priya…

I really liked the time we spent together.

It felt real. Would love to meet again — maybe dinner? :)"

He hovered. Then tapped Send.

The message whooshed into the void. A second passed. Then five. Then ten.

He stared. The typing dots danced… then disappeared. Then reappeared. Then stopped again. Then… buzz.

**Priya:**

"Would love that 💖

Tomorrow night?"

Raghav let out a breath he didn't know he was holding. He grinned like a twelve-year-old who just learned to whistle.

He sent a reply to Priya: "Yes! That works perfectly for me too"

**FlirtBuddy** (dropping into the chat with a disco gif):

*"LET'S GOOOOOO 🔥*

*You're in, buddy!*

*This calls for… the celebratory shuffle."*

**Raghav:**

"What celebratory shuffle?"

**FlirtBuddy:**

*"Check this playlist I just dropped into your Music app:*

*Songs for Nervous Romantics Who Just Got a Yes™*

*First up: ♫ Otha Sollala from Aadukalam ♫ — raw, real, rhythm-in-your-bones kinda joy.*

*Now, dance like your overthinking just went on vacation."*

It started with that earthy folk rhythm — playful, chaotic, alive.

Raghav laughed. And he danced — not perfectly, not gracefully — but like someone alive in his body again. Like someone who finally felt worthy of romance. Like someone who had just taken the first step toward something real.

He wasn't a simulation anymore.

He was Raghav.

He was awkward, sincere, confused, curious — and slowly, finally, becoming bold.

And in his pocket, FlirtBuddy winked quietly, already preparing the next level — because love was no longer a concept.

It was a story.

And Raghav was starting to write his.

## Chapter 6 — The Kiss That Entangled Us

It was a Saturday morning. The kind that started slow, with mist curling gently against the windows and Bangalore traffic taking its time to stir.

Raghav had returned home early after temple duties — a morning puja at the sannidhi, a few quiet account entries, and a content walk back with steaming filter coffee in hand.

But today, something felt different. He was lighter. Brighter.

Last night, just before bed, Priya had said she'd like to meet again — a soft, "Yes, I'd like that :)" in response to a message he nervously typed. It wasn't a plan yet — but it was an opening. A doorway.

Now, sitting by the window in his shorts, the morning sun casting a warm glow on the tiles, he couldn't stop smiling. Her warmth wasn't just politeness — it was possibility.

The simulations with FlirtBuddy had given him confidence. Rehearsed conversations, emotional loops, scenario trees — they helped. But this was no script. No safe simulation loop. This was real. Real people. Real feelings.

And this time, he wanted to show up as himself.

He opened his phone and typed:

**Raghav:**

"Morning :) Just letting you know… I'm really looking forward to tonight."

A pause. Then the reply buzzed back:

**Priya:**

"Me too :)"

He waited a beat. Then followed up:

**Raghav:**

"Hey... I was thinking we should meet somewhere we can talk... without distractions."

**Priya:**

"Sounds perfect... Do you have a place in mind?"

**Raghav:**

"How about Street Storyss in Indiranagar? Nice food... quiet corner seats... I think it might be just what we need."

**Priya:**

"Street Storyss... I've been meaning to try it! Okay, it's a date. 7 pm?"

**Raghav:**

"See you there! "

Priya eased into her own version of the day. A casual appointment at Bounce for a trim and a quick blow-dry — nothing fancy, but enough to feel fresh. As the stylist sectioned her hair, she stared into the mirror, playing with possible versions of herself. "It's just dinner," she told herself. But when she lingered over her small gold earrings later — the ones that made her feel quietly confident — it said otherwise.

By noon, the city had shaken off its sleep. The weekend was in full swing.

Priya returned home, hair still holding the scent of salon mist, playlist humming softly, carefully laying out her wine-colored wrap dress. She debated between flats and heels.

Raghav, freshly showered and staring at his wardrobe as if it held philosophical meaning, finally settled on a black jacket and a dark grey tee.

The night hadn't even begun. But something already felt alive. Like the world was gently tilting forward — toward something waiting.

He zipped through the streets on his Ather 450X, the quiet

hum of the electric motor cutting cleanly through the chaotic rhythm of a Bangalore Saturday night. The city was alive — and nowhere more than Indiranagar.

As he turned onto 100 Feet Road, he could feel the mood shift.

Indiranagar was glowing.

Strings of fairy lights hung like constellations between palm trees and lamp posts. The sidewalks brimmed with Bengaluru's weekend pulse — fashionably late twenty-somethings hopping between microbreweries and rooftop cafés, their laughter riding the breeze. Music spilled from every corner — the smooth brass of live jazz at BFlat, a retro Fleetwood Mac cover at Pecos, bass drops from an EDM set upstairs at Loft 38. The scent of rain-dampened soil mingled with the steam of hot momo and clove-laced cocktails.

He slowed his Ather as he passed familiar landmarks — Toit's waiting crowd, Glen's Bakehouse glowing soft yellow, the forever-busy Corner House with couples sharing Death by Chocolate like it was a date ritual.

The street wasn't traffic — it was theatre.

And for once, Raghav didn't feel like a spectator.

The simulations, the awkward rehearsals, the physics jokes — they had all led here. He wasn't in some dusty corridor of the temple. He wasn't fumbling through his head.

He was here. Riding smoothly. Jacket zipped. Nervous, but ready.

As Street Storyss came into view — its rustic wood-and-glass exterior lit with warm orange lamps and strung bulbs swaying slightly in the breeze — he slowed, turned off the ignition, and stepped off the bike.

He removed his helmet, smoothed his hair, and smiled to himself.

This was no longer about perfection.

It was about presence.

Through the glass, he saw her.

She was already there.

Sitting by the corner window.

Phone placed face-down. Hands folded gently in her lap.

Looking outward, rain tapped softly against the glass beside her.

Draped in a wine-colored wrap dress, her hair freshly curled and catching the restaurant's amber lights, she looked like the very pause in a film before something beautiful begins.

His stomach flipped.

He whispered under his breath — not a prayer, not a line — just:

"There you are."

And pushed the door open — into warmth, into light, into her.

He walked towards her table, heart pacing in rhythm with the soft jazz playing in the background, and slipped into the seat across from her.

**Raghav:**

"You're looking wonderful tonight."

He said that with no hesitation. Like it was just the truth.

**Priya** (tilting her head):

"And you… that black jacket's making you look almost… handsome."

**Raghav** (teasing):

"Almost?"

**Priya** (smiling):

"Don't get used to it."

They both smiled, and the space between them felt lighter — the kind of easy air that only comes when you've each been seen.

**Priya:**

"You've been here before… got any favorites?"

**Raghav** (smiling shyly):

"Yeah, the Pumpkin Ghee Podi Blue Cheese with Scallion Chilli Parota — it's got this surprising sweetness from the pumpkin, with a little kick from the chili."

**Priya** (teasing):

"Love the way you said that."

**Raghav** (chuckling):

"Maybe. For mains, the Lotan Chole with Imli Chutney and Mint Kulcha — tangy, comforting, and the kulcha has just enough bite. Like a warm hug you didn't know you needed."

**Priya:**

"I'm sold. But I want to add the Masala Tofu Tikka — tofu deserves some love, too, right? And something to drink?"

**Raghav** (grinning):

"Definitely. Drinks?"

**Priya:**

"Rose Lemonade — sweet and floral."

**Raghav:**

"Lemongrass Ginger Cooler — zingy, like this night."

The waiter took their order and disappeared, leaving a soft silence filled with quiet smiles.

The dishes arrived, steaming and fragrant.

Raghav plated some of the Pumpkin Ghee Podi Blue Cheese with Scallion Chilli Parota onto their plates and took a bite, eyes meeting Priya's.

**Raghav:**

"Every time I have it, it feels like a little celebration."

**Priya** (smiling as she tasted it):

"That's really good. Unexpected, but it works."

She took some Masala Tofu Tikka from the shared plate.

**Priya:**

"This tofu is smoky and spicy — like it has a story. I'm

guessing you do too."

**Raghav** (chuckling softly):

"Maybe. But I'm more interested in hearing yours."

As they moved on to the mains, sharing bites of the Lotan Chole with Imli Chutney and Mint Kulcha, Priya's curiosity got the better of her.

**Priya:**

"You seem to really enjoy physics. What is it about it that you like?"

**Raghav** (smiling softly, thinking):

"Physics feels like the universe's way of telling its story. It's this invisible language behind everything — from why these pumpkin tastes sweet to how light dances through these windows."

**Priya** (nodding thoughtfully):

"So it's like understanding the magic behind the everyday?"

**Raghav:**

"Exactly. Like gravity — you don't see it, but it's always there, holding us down, making sure we don't float away. Kind of like the small, unseen forces in life that keep us grounded."

**Priya** (eyes sparkling):

"I like that. So, are you saying I'm one of those forces keeping you grounded tonight?"

**Raghav** (cheeks warming as he looked up):

"Maybe. You definitely have some gravitational pull."

They both laughed softly, the connection between them growing warmer.

Priya smiles, tracing the rim of her glass.

**Priya:**

"I don't know how useful all this is in our mundane, day-to-day lives… but the physics does make us more curious — and it's fun to see the connections."

After a pause, Raghav leans back slightly, a gentle smile

playing on his lips.

**Raghav:**

"Feynman once said, 'Physics is like sex. Not for the result. But for the experience.'"

Priya laughs, a mix of surprise and delight lighting her eyes.

**Priya:**

"That's probably the best way anyone's ever described science — and maybe life too."

She leans back in her chair, playful glint in her eyes.

**Priya:**

"What about dessert?"

Raghav grins, every word falling like a line of poetry.

**Raghav:**

"The Rose Kheer — sweet, floral, delicate. Like the perfect note to end a song."

He catches the waiter's attention with a polite wave.

**Raghav:**

"One Rose Kheer, please."

Priya laughs softly, tucking a strand of hair behind her ear, and for a moment, the world narrows to just the two of them.

Just then, the rose kheer arrived, its pink glow and delicate fragrance curling into the space between them.

Priya dipped her spoon first, tasting it with a small hum of delight.

**Priya** (smiling):

"Oh wow… this is dangerous. Sweet, creamy, and just enough rose to make it feel like poetry."

Raghav followed, savoring a spoonful. The cool richness melted on his tongue, and he couldn't help but smile wider than usual.

**Raghav** (softly):

"Maybe this is gravity too — everything pulling us toward something sweeter."

She looked at him, spoon paused in midair.

**Priya:**

"So this? This dinner, this moment… It's about the experience?"

**Raghav:**

"Exactly. Letting it unfold. Moment by moment."

And just like that — they slipped out of theory and into something tender, real, and undeniably theirs.

Outside, the Bangalore night had turned misty again. They stepped into the chill, walking slowly beneath streetlights that spilled golden puddles across the sidewalk, each step echoing like part of a scene neither wanted to end.

Their knuckles brushed. Once. Twice. And then, without ceremony, their fingers intertwined. For Raghav, it felt less like a choice and more like gravity — the kind you couldn't escape, even if you wanted to.

He paused. Lifted her hand. Pressed a kiss against her knuckles, soft and reverent, as if they were something sacred. His heart, usually so anxious and overthinking, was strangely steady — like the equations finally balanced.

Priya stopped. Turned to him. The mist haloed around her, streetlight catching in her eyes. And then, with a certainty that startled them both, she closed the space between their lips.

A warm kiss. Gentle. Unhurried.

And in that moment, Raghav felt time dissolve — no theories, no fears, no variables left to solve. Just the clarity of her mouth against his, tender and absolute.

**Priya** (mischievous, breathless):

"Did Feynman say… a kiss is not for the result, but for the experience?"

**Raghav** (a nervous, happy mess, whispered):

"Exactly."

**Raghav** (gently):

"Hey… want me to drop you back?"

**Priya** (smiling):

"Only if you promise not to drive like a temple priest."

He laughed, unlocking his Ather 450X. She climbed on behind him, arms wrapping tightly around his waist — not just for balance, but with quiet intent.

FlirtBuddy's last whisper echoed in his head:

*"Connection — not perfection."*

He tapped the console. Switched to Warp Mode.

The motor purred. The city blurred.

She held him close, fingers threading into his jacket as if letting go was impossible, her body pressed to his like she meant it. They rode in silence through Indiranagar's glowing lanes — cafés murmuring, scooters gliding over puddles, music curling from rooftops. The city seemed to lean in, giving them a world that was theirs alone.

As they neared the end of 12th Main, Priya tapped his shoulder gently and leaned in close.

**Priya** (mischievous):

"Ice cream?"

He turned slightly and smiled. No questions.

They pulled up at Corner House, still open for late-night romantics and dessert loyalists. Inside, a few couples huddled under dim yellow lights, the glass fogged from the mix of rain and chocolate.

They ordered one Death By Chocolate, two spoons.

Outside, they found a bench beneath a narrow awning. The drizzle whispered around them. The spoon clinked against the cup.

**Priya** (teasing):

"Do you eat your ice cream slow… or like a science experiment?"

**Raghav** (grinning):

"Slow. Controlled. With great respect for temperature gradients."

**Priya:**

"Good. People who rush dessert can't be trusted."

She took the first bite, then passed the cup to him. Their fingers brushed — the third time that evening. This one lingered.

**Raghav** (softly):

"I can't believe you kissed me."

**Priya:**

"You kissed my hand first, remember? Physics made the first move."

**Raghav** (smiling):

"Right. Quantum Flirtation."

**Priya:**

"Exactly. A minor but irreversible event."

They laughed, softer now. The drizzle framed them in a kind of quiet, timeless bubble.

**Raghav** (quietly):

"Tonight feels like… discovering something I didn't know I was allowed to feel."

She looked at him for a beat — no teasing now, just presence.

**Priya:**

"You didn't just feel it. You created it."

They finished the ice cream slowly. No hurry. No rules.

When they stood again, she slipped her hand into his without asking.

**Priya:**

"Ready to warp?"

**Raghav:**

"Let's fly."

They rode past Lalbagh into south Bangalore, the roads

now quiet, slick with mist. Her cheek rested lightly against his back. She didn't speak. She didn't need to.

By the time they reached Jayanagar, the city had curled into sleep.

She stepped off, adjusting her dress.

**Priya** (smiling):

"Thank you. Warp Mode suits you."

He nodded — cheeks aching from smiling — then turned and rode off, the drizzle returning like applause.

Back at his house, Raghav parked the Ather under the tin-roof portico. The night had stretched just long enough to feel like a dream, but short enough to want again.

Upstairs, he kicked off his shoes, changed into his softest grey shorts and faded Doppler effect T-shirt — his go-to when the world finally made sense.

He fell back onto his mattress, hair still damp from the ride, the scent of her strawberry shampoo somehow still clinging to his breath.

He opened the FlirtBuddy app, thumbs trembling with joy.

**Raghav:**

"It happened. We kissed.

Ice cream. Warp Mode. She held me.

I think something beautiful might be beginning."

A beat. Then FlirtBuddy replied:

**FlirtBuddy:**

*"Okay, roomie — I'm literally bouncing off our shared metaphorical walls right now.*

*Dopamine levels: 9000.*

*We have to dance this off. No arguments. Shirt optional."*

Raghav laughed out loud.

Then — a notification blinked.

Now Playing: ♫ "Everybody (Backstreet's Back)" ♫

**FlirtBuddy:**

*"Because if tonight had a soundtrack... It's this.*

*This is your cue to pretend you're in a boy band and point at the mirror dramatically."*

Raghav got up, barefoot, loose-limbed, still dizzy with adrenaline. He spun, moonwalked, pointed dramatically at his reflection, and sang aloud:

"Am I original? YEAHHH!"

His phone buzzed mid-chorus.

**Priya:**

"Hey :)

Just wanted to say... tonight was wonderful. I haven't felt like this in a long time. Sleep sweet."

He paused, heart still racing — but for softer reasons now.

He read it twice. Then replied to Priya.

**Raghav:**

"Good night, Priya.

Somewhere in this vast universe, two particles just moved closer.

I'll hold onto that entanglement... until morning finds us again."

**FlirtBuddy:**

*"Okay. I'm emotional now.*

*We need to bottle this night and release it as a scent called Intimacy 101."*

Raghav curled into his mattress, phone still lit beside him, the Backstreet Boys playing faintly in the background.

And just like that, Raghav and FlirtBuddy — roommates, wingmen, and co-pilots of this strange human experiment called love — danced quietly into sleep.

Entangled. Not just in theory. In breath, in memory, in sleep.

## Chapter 7 — Sundays Are for Stories

Sunday mornings in the Shastrigal household moved at a different rhythm. The usual clang of vessels and chant of slokas was softer, slower. The pressure cooker let out just one hiss before pausing, as if even it didn't want to rush the day. The windows stayed open longer, letting in a breeze that smelled faintly of jasmine and fresh curry leaves. Somewhere in the background, a radio played a sleepy old Carnatic raga — not loud, just enough to hum through the house like memory.

Jayalakshmi Mami was at the stove in her cotton saree, her feet bare on the cool mosaic tiles. She wasn't in a hurry today — the Pooris puffed up one by one, golden and crisp, each flipped with the kind of satisfaction that only a Sunday morning offered. The Channa simmered beside her, thick with spice and slow intention.

Raghav walked in, freshly bathed, wearing soft cotton shorts and a plain white T-shirt.

He looked rested — and something else, too. Lighter. As if the air itself had unclenched overnight.

From the dining table, the scent of roasted jeera and ghee hung like a promise.

**Jayalakshmi Mami** (calling out, voice easy):

"Raghava! Breakfast's ready! Come before the pooris go shy."

**Raghav** (walking in, towel around his neck, hair still damp):

"Mmm.... You made poori-channa?"

**Jayalakshmi** (smiling, unfazed):

"Sunday tradition, kanna. Weekdays are for rules. Sundays are for indulgence."

Raghav settled at the dining table beside his father. The morning light poured in diagonally across the table, warming the steel tumblers and casting a quiet glow over the scene.

Srinivasan Shastrigal had set aside his newspaper, unusually attentive to the smells wafting in from the kitchen. He picked up a poori and, slowly and with precision, dipped it into the channa.

**Srinivasan** (adjusting his glasses, looking over the edge of the newspaper):

"What's with the grin, da? Did Gill hit a century I missed?"

**Raghav** (grinning):

"Nothing Appa"

Jayalakshmi Mami walked in with a fresh plate of pooris, playfully swatting at the two of them with a tissue before setting the plate down. Still chuckling, she placed a puffed poori onto each of their plates, as if serving both food and joy in the same breath.

**Jayalakshmi:**

"Don't be cryptic. It's that Priya girl, isn't it?"

**Raghav** (half-laughing, half-resigned):

"Amma…"

**Srinivasan** (mildly amused):

"Is it going well?"

**Raghav** (quietly, picking at a poori):

"Yeah. We've been talking. It feels… natural. Easy. I'll keep you posted."

**Jayalakshmi** (nodding approvingly):

"She has a good presence of mind. And she helped clear the plates without being asked.

That says something."

**Srinivasan** (folding his napkin with precision):

"Marriage is not about show. It's about habits. Watching. Listening. Being able to sit in silence without discomfort."

**Raghav** (smiling):

"We haven't tried silence yet. But… I'll let you know."

They ate in content quiet for a while, the only sounds being the crunch of pooris and the soft bubbling of a second round of coffee on the stove.

By late morning, the swing in the Shastrigal hall creaked gently under Raghav. Half-scrolling, half-dreaming, he looked like someone still savoring the aftertaste of cardamom and possibility—when the phone buzzed. It was WhatsApp notifications:

**Group: Malleshwaram Heroes™**

👑 Since 2008. Still undefeated in excuses, overthinking, and one breakup band support.

**Rahul:**

"Boys. Big Brewsky. 6 pm. I've got gossip and Gopi's paying. 🤑"

**Gopi:**

"Whaaa—?"

**Rahul:**

"He lost in poker last night. Verbal contract. Witnessed by Tea shop Nagesh Uncle, who now considers himself the notary public of Malleshwaram."

**Vijay:**

"Done. If Gopi's paying, I'm ordering nachos for emotional support"

**Vijay:**

"Raghav in? Or is he still decoding Sanskrit flirting protocols like it's the Da Vinci Code?"

**Raghav** (typing with a smirk):

"Coming. 6 sharp. Bringing my Rigveda for backup."

**Gopi:**

"Tell us everything, Mr Entangled. 😏"

**Rahul:**

"Can't wait to see him blush. Somebody get a blood pressure monitor."

**Raghav** (grinning as he sent):

"Just don't expect death-by-channa level drama."

**Vijay:**

"Fair. But if you kissed her, you're buying fries. And maybe a round of shots for the pub."

**Raghav** (pausing, then):

"See you at 6. Long story. Bring tissues. And Gopi's wallet."

He tossed the phone aside, stretched like a cat, and smiled quietly to himself.

**Byg Brewsky, Hennur**

By 6 PM, Bangalore's amber evening had wrapped itself around Hennur, and at **Byg Brewsky,** their chosen sanctum. The koi pond shimmered under the fairy lights. Laughter drifted from table to table like incense. Trays of grilled pineapple, beer-battered mushrooms, and sky-high cocktails floated by as if choreographed.

Raghav arrived first — wearing his favourite Marvel Hulk T-shirt, hair still a little tousled, like he'd just stepped out of a really good dream and wasn't quite ready to let it go. He slid into the high stool, the late-evening breeze tousling his sleeves, and ordered a Virgin Mojito. As the mint clinked against the ice, he took his first slow sip — smiling to himself like someone carrying a quiet secret.

Gopi thudded into the seat next to him, wearing his favourite faded "Messi > Physics" T-shirt, eyes already scanning the koi pond like he was solving a puzzle.

**Gopi:**

"You look suspiciously happy for a man drinking crushed

mint and lime."

**Raghav** (deadpan):

"Mint is underrated."

Moments later, **Vijay** and **Rahul** arrived together — one with a messenger bag, the other with a swagger that suggested an imaginary fan following.

**Vijay** wore a black tee that said "Design is Thinking Made Visual" in clean Helvetica. His glasses slid down his nose like an afterthought, and his usual half-beanie made him look like a Pinterest board on legs.

**Rahul**, meanwhile, strutted in wearing a faded red T-shirt with "Namma Ooru, Namma Beat" printed in bold, brush-stroke lettering — part of his self-funded Kannada rap merch line. He wore it like a badge, the cotton slightly stretched from a recent performance at a basement gig.

**Rahul** (plopping into the seat):

"Cheers for beer and boys doing boy things."

They bumped fists and settled in.

The waiter came by, tab in hand, and the boys barely glanced at the menu — this was a ritual, after all.

— Gopi went straight for a tall glass of wheat beer. "No bitter surprises," he said. "Just like my engineering career."

— Vijay ordered a crisp IPA, already half-lost in the design of the label. "I drink by font. This one's got character."

— Rahul, in peak artiste mode, chose a Guava Chilli Vodka Punch. "For the heat. Creativity needs discomfort."

— And for the table, they called in the classics: fully loaded nachos, beer-battered mushrooms with paprika aioli, and — after a moment's debate — a portion of peri-peri paneer tikka "for balance."

As the orders were punched on the tab, an old-school guitar riff filled the air — Led Zeppelin. Maybe Deep Purple. The kind of music that made heads nod unconsciously and conversations take a nostalgic turn.

**Vijay** (grinned):

"They always play our era when we land up. Like the DJ's contractually obliged to honor our dad-bod playlist."

**Rahul** (raised his glass):

"To loyalty. And loud choruses nobody asked for."

Plates arrived like familiar friends, the air rich with spices, jokes, and the rhythm of stories only old friends could afford to tell slowly.

**Gopi:**

"Okay, let's not waste time. Who's the girl, and why is Raghav looking like he's been blessed by Saraswati and Lakshmi both?"

**Rahul:**

"Bro, he didn't just smile when I asked. He gave me a Rumi smile. Something's cooking."

**Raghav** (shrugging, but lips curving):

"Let's just say… we've met a few times now. Her name is Priya."

He casually pulled out his phone, tapped into the gallery, and turned the screen toward the group. A candid shot — Priya mid-laugh, hair caught in the breeze, eyes half-squinting at the sun. The kind of picture that didn't try too hard but somehow lingered.

**Rahul** (leaning in, dramatic gasp):

"Broooo. She's stunning. Like… bookstore in a rainstorm stunning."

**Vijay** (whistling):

"She has That Smile. The one that ruins checklists and restarts playlists."

**Gopi** (nodding with mock solemnity):

"Keep her. It can't get better. Also, she has intelligent eyes energy. I approve."

A beat.

**Gopi** (mock gasp):

"Not just the 'girl-seeing' protocol? Repeat meetings? What's the equation?"

**Raghav:**

"No equations. Just… symmetry. She makes me feel like I don't have to explain myself all the time. You know?"

**Rahul:**

"Explain da, what did you do? Dinner? Movie? A romantic temple walk?"

**Gopi** (dramatic eyebrow wiggle):

"Be honest, da. Was there... contact?"

**Raghav** (sipping virgin mojito, playing it cool):

"There may have been… a moment."

**Rahul** (nearly chokes on his beer):

"A MOMENT? What is this, Ramayana? Speak like a modern man!"

**Vijay** (grinning):

"Bro. Define moment. Like… are we talking hand touch, cheek brush, or full soundtrack kiss?"

**Raghav** (smiling, eyes distant):

"Let's just say… something unspoken finally spoke."

The boys fell briefly quiet. Then—

**Rahul** (softly dramatic):

"You kissed her."

**Raghav** (nodding, slowly):

"Under the mist. After dessert. Soft, real... not planned."

**Gopi** (raising his beer):

"Now that's the kind of dessert I respect."

**Vijay** (teasing):

"Tell me you didn't drop a Feynman quote during the kiss."

**Raghav** (grinning):

"Actually… she did."

For a moment, no one spoke. The boys just stared, blinking — as if trying to process what they'd heard.

**Gopi:**

"She dropped a physics quote?!"

**Raghav:**

"She said, 'Was that kiss for the result… or the experience?'" (smiles, voice lower)

"And I said… 'Exactly.'"

The table explodes in hoots and whistles.

**Rahul** (banging the table):

"KEEP HER."

**Vijay:**

"Bro! If she's quoting Feynman during a kiss, that's not a girl — that's a Nobel Prize wrapped in eyeliner."

**Gopi:**

"No more analysis, da. This is it. Tie the thali. It can't get any better for you"

They all laugh, raising their glasses like four slightly drunk philosophers.

**Rahul:**

"To Priya. May she continue quoting Feynman and confusing temple boys forever."

Meanwhile, across the city, as golden afternoon light slipped past beer mugs and bromance at Big Brewsky…

**Champaca Café, Off Queens Road**

A different kind of Sunday unfolded at Champaca Café, nestled like a quiet secret between the trees off Queens Road. The kind of place you didn't stumble upon — you found it when you were ready to slow down.

Books leaned sleepily on tall wooden shelves. Bougainvillea spilled over railings. Hanging plants swayed lazily in the filtered sun, and somewhere in the background, someone flipped through an old Gulzar paperback while waiting for warm banana cake. The terrace smelled of filter coffee, rain-dried cushions, and the faint hint of coconut oil from someone's morning bath. Conversations didn't echo — they lingered like steam.

**Priya** sat barefoot in a low cane chair, one leg tucked under her, the other lazily swaying to the rhythm of rustling leaves. Her phone lay untouched. Her cold coffee sat sweating onto a coaster printed with a Tagore quote.

She wore a soft blue chikankari kurta — the kind that floated when she walked, the fabric holding sunlight in its weave. Paired with cotton culottes and tiny silver anklets that chimed faintly when she moved, she looked like a page from a poem written just after a kiss. No eyeliner today, just lip balm and that unmistakable post-kiss quiet glow that no brand could manufacture.

Across from her, **Aarushi** stirred her turmeric latte with clinical intensity. She wore an ivory linen kurta that said, I'm not trying, but I will still outdress you. Hoops in the size of bangles and an expression that could hold both sarcasm and wisdom in the same breath.

Aarushi had been Priya's closest friend since college — dorm beds pushed together during heartbreaks, mid-semester crisis phone calls, shared Google Sheets of red flags, and voice notes that always began with "okay, don't judge me, but…" She was the one who once said, with the kind of clarity that left a mark, "If it's not making you laugh or making you grow, it's not love — it's just a slow allergy." Priya had listened. Mostly.

And they were still a team — not just in the nostalgic, remember-our-dorm-days way, but in the everyday battlefield of adulthood. Now they worked side by side: Priya, the UX designer who could turn chaos into clean, intuitive flows; and

Aarushi, the strategist who could slice through any problem with logic sharp enough to whistle. In meetings, Priya sketched wireframes while Aarushi translated them into pitches; in crises, they traded glances like coded messages; and on long workdays, their old rhythm returned as effortlessly as breathing. People in the office joked that they operated like one organism with two caffeine sources. The friendship had survived love, career chaos, and several suspiciously dramatic breakups — and the fact that they still chose each other every morning felt like its own quiet miracle.

Now, Aarushi looked up, narrowing her eyes with playful suspicion.

**Aarushi** (without looking up):

"So, you have this stupid post-kiss glow."

**Priya** (smiling, mock offended):

"It's not stupid. It's… mildly radioactive."

**Aarushi:**

"I see. You're glowing. Like Diwali came early and brought feelings, 'I like this boy.' Spill. What's he like? Beard oil? Crypto bros? Or those ones who say 'dogs over people' in dating bios?"

**Priya** (laughs):

"None of that. He's… gentle. Thoughtful. Very quiet. Not trying to impress me. Just… listening."

**Aarushi** (raising an eyebrow):

"Listening is rare. Do go on."

She scrolled through her gallery, found the one she had quietly taken — Raghav half-turned away, backlit by warm light at Street Storyss, looking like he didn't know he was being seen.

"Here. That's him."

**Priya:**

"He's a temple accountant."

**Aarushi** (leaning in):

"Oof. Okay. That forehead definitely files temple balance sheets."

**Priya** (smiling):

"And a Sanskrit nerd. Also... he says things like how quantum entanglement reminds him of human connection."

**Aarushi:**

"Stop. You've found Bangalore's last poetic boy. Protect him at all costs."

**Priya** (quietly):

"Yeah. A poem with a scooter and perfectly awkward smiles."

They sat for a moment, letting the scent of fresh banana cake and filter coffee drift around them.

**Aarushi** (watching her):

"You like him."

**Priya** (softly):

"I do."

**Aarushi:**

"But?"

**Priya** (long pause):

"I think I've dated noise for too long. The bold ones, the charming ones, the ambitious ones. This is... quiet. This feels like space to breathe. I just... don't know if I trust that yet."

**Aarushi:**

"You don't have to. Not yet. Just... show up. That's enough for now."

**Priya:**

"Last night felt like a movie. But not the kind where everything is burning. More like... when someone fixes your tea without asking."

**Aarushi:**

"And now you're scared it'll vanish?"

**Priya:**

"Yeah."

**Aarushi** (gently):

"Priya, your fire is beautiful. But maybe this time, let the warmth in, too."

They shared a slice of caramel banana cake in silence, breaking it carefully with spoons, as if it were some tender ritual.

**Aarushi:**

"What did you talk about?"

**Priya:**

"Physics. Feynman. Comfort food. Our fears."

**Aarushi:**

"And kissing?"

**Priya** (smiling):

"It just happened. It wasn't planned. We were walking, he kissed my hand… and then I leaned in. It was soft. Certain."

**Aarushi:**

"God, I'm rooting for him already."

**Priya:**

"I didn't think I'd feel this way so soon. I usually take time. Like… filters and evaluations and background checks."

**Aarushi** (softly):

"Maybe the checklist isn't the test. Maybe it's just noticing how you feel around him. Do you feel more yourself, or less?"

**Priya** (after a beat):

"More. Weirdly more. Like, I don't have to be clever. Just… me."

Aarushi smiled, then stretched.

**Aarushi:**

"Okay. That's it. I'm officially giving him a provisional green flag."

**Priya:**

"What does that even mean?"

**Aarushi:**

"He's on probation. If he buys you bad coffee or sends you forwarded good morning messages, I revoke it."

**Priya** (grinning):

"Fair."

As they stood to leave, Priya's phone buzzed. It was from Raghav on WhatsApp. A photo. A picture of him, Rahul, Vijay and Gopi — clinking glasses and grinning at Big Brewsky.

**Raghav:**

"Today was good. I told them about you."

**Priya** (without overthinking):

"I told my best friend too. She's officially rooting for you. Probationary, but still." 😄

Later that night, with the fan humming above her and her hair still damp from a post-walk shower, Priya curled up in bed. The windows were open, the city breathing in and out. She stared at her phone for a moment, debating, then finally sent a text message on WhatsApp:

**Priya:**

"Hey. You free to talk? Or are you on warp mode, saving the world?"

The reply came instantly.

**Raghav:**

"Saving the world can wait. Talking to you > everything."

They slipped into a warm, easy banter that felt like silk over skin.

**Priya:**

"What are you wearing, Mr Quantum Flirtation?"

**Raghav:**

"Plain grey tee. Pyjama pants with stars on them. You?"

**Priya:**

"Blue kurta. No eyeliner. Lip balm. Messy bun."

**Raghav:**

"Dangerous combination. That glow from yesterday is still illegal."

**Priya:**

"You didn't say that last night."

**Raghav:**

"I couldn't say much with your lips doing the talking."

A pause. Three dots.

**Priya:**

"Careful. You're becoming smooth."

**Raghav:**

"No. Just honest. And maybe still tasting a little bit of you in my dreams."

**Priya:**

"Raghav!"

**Raghav:**

"Sorry. Physics made me say it."

**Priya:**

"Are you blushing?"

**Raghav:**

"Fully. Face is basically a thermal map now."

She giggled into her pillow, biting her lip.

**Priya:**

"Okay. One question before sleep."

**Raghav:**

"Go."

**Priya:**

"If I kissed you again right now… what would you do?"

**Raghav:**

"Not breathe. Not blink. Just stay there. Until the stars got jealous."

**Priya:**

"Uff."

**Raghav:**

"You asked."

**Priya:**

"I did. And I'm smiling like an idiot."

**Raghav:**

"Same. Shall we… fall asleep stupidly happy now?"

**Priya:**

"Mmm. Goodnight, quantum boy."

**Raghav:**

"Sleep well, Priya. If dreams start feeling too real, blame entanglement."

She sent a heart emoji back and placed the phone beside her on the soft, creased bedsheet, the message still glowing faintly on the screen. A string of fairy lights blinked above her bookshelf, casting golden freckles on the wall. She curled back into her cushion — oversized, faded, and familiar — the kind that remembers your shape.

Her fingers brushed her lips, unconsciously, as if trying to replay the smile that had bloomed there. Outside, a single leaf rustled against the windowpane. Inside, her heart was doing cartwheels she'd never confess.

Whatever this was — it was beginning to feel like the kind of story she might actually believe in.

In another part of the city, Raghav lay, staring at his ceiling fan, one hand behind his head, the other still holding the phone as if it were her hand.

They weren't in the same room. But somehow, they were curled up in the same space between thoughts, entangled — like fingers not yet touching, but already memorising the map of each other.

# Chapter 8 — Week of good night messages

"Sometimes, in the middle of an ordinary life, love gives us a fairy tale."

Neither Raghav nor Priya would usually take that seriously. Too saccharine. Too predictable. The kind of thing printed on the back of a wedding card, with golden roses and glitter fonts.

But this week, it lingered—not as cliché, but as truth. Soft, uninvited, undeniable.

## Monday — The First Good Morning

### 4:59 AM — Malleshwaram, Bengaluru

Before the first suprabhātam curled into the morning air, Raghav was already awake.

The city was still dreaming, but he wasn't. His body moved in rhythm — brushing teeth with cold tap water, folding panche (veshti) with reverence, lighting the brass lamp in his puja nook.

But something was different today.

Even as he sprinkled tulsi water and whispered slokas to a still-sleeping dawn, his mind wasn't entirely here. His fingers hovered just a second too long over the diya. His ears were tuned not to the shankha echo but to a vibration that hadn't yet come.

### 5:45 AM

Rituals done. Coffee brewed. Phone unlocked.

**[1 message]**

**Priya:**

"Good morning, sleepy Sanskrit scholar ○ Hope you dreamed of me... or pumpkin cheese subji. Either is acceptable."

Raghav smiled into his tumbler.

**Raghav:**

"Woke up with Vishnu Sahasranamam. Now upgraded to you. You > the Rig Veda."

**Priya:**

"Don't blaspheme, Raghav Shastrigal. But… noted. I'm somewhere between the Upanishads and pillow right now."

And just like that —

Monday began. Not with alarms.

But with affection typed in sleepy eyes and sent across town like the day's first prayer.

**9:14 AM — Jayanagar**

Priya sat cross-legged in her home-office nook, hair damp, cheeks still flushed from a quick bath. Her Figma screen glitched. Or maybe it was her heart.

**Ping.**

**Raghav:**

"Why do I suddenly want to learn UX? Just to build you an app that says 'you're beautiful' every time you open it."

She laughed, biting her lip.

**Priya:**

"Make it blink and crash like old-school Flash sites. And say: 'Welcome, Priya. Server of love is live.'"

**Raghav:**

"Done. Every error message will say: 'Error 404: Distance Not Found.'"

She almost spilled her drink. The warmth of her laugh lingered in the air.

**12:41 PM — Temple Office**

The cat under Raghav's desk stretched. So did he. But his attention was elsewhere.

**Raghav (typing):**

"Today's to-do list:

1. Finish accounts
2. Avoid stepping on a cat
3. Think of your smile for no reason
4. Do Step 3. Repeatedly"

**Priya:**

"I'm printing that and sticking it on your forehead."

He chuckled. But a small wave of doubt crept in — a flicker, barely a thought.

Raghav opens the Flirtbuddy app on his phone:

"FlirtBuddy, are you there? Am I… overdoing it?"

A familiar soft glow blinked.

The voice was velvet with mischief, dipped in stardust and algorithmic truth.

**FlirtBuddy:**

*"You're in love, Raghav. The body wants closeness. The mind fears too much. Let's find the sweet spot."*

*"Science says desire thrives in unpredictability. Flirting isn't pressure. It's play."*

**Raghav:**

"She's teasing me. I want to tease her back. Gently. Like... physics in a sari."

**FlirtBuddy** (smirking):

*"Try this: 'Do you know what my favourite interface is? Your mind. The UI is stunning. And the UX… devastating.'"*

**Raghav:**

"Damn."

He copied and pasted it and hit send, like pulling a trigger.

A minute later:

**Priya:**
"Who are you and what have you done with Shy Boy?"
**Raghav:**
"Let's just say… I'm under divine upgrade."

**8:18 PM – Balconies**

She video called during dinner, in her oversized "Beats Before Deadlines" tee, scooping curd rice like it was edible nostalgia.

He answered instantly. The lighting on his face was soft, golden. Like her smile had stayed with him all day.

**Priya:**
"You didn't tell me you have dimples. That's criminal withholding of information."
**Raghav** (adjusting camera):
"They only show up when I'm looking at you. Conditional formatting."
**Priya:**
"RAGHAV."

**10:32 PM — Raghav's Room**

Lights off. Phone glowing like a low moon in his palm.

He blinked into the darkness. Opens the glow of the FlirtBuddy app.

**Raghav:**
"FlirtBuddy… I want to wish her goodnight. But something real. Poetic. Is that okay?"

The AI stirred.

**FlirtBuddy:**
*"I'm not here to write your story, da. Just to help you say it better."*
*"Your words. Your heart. I'll polish the punctuation."*

**Together**, they wrote:

*"Goodnight, Priya.*

*May your dreams unfold like morning light on temple steps. Slow. Certain.*

*And if I appear in them... blame it on quantum probability."*

He hit send.

One breath. Two.

**Priya (typing):**

"You're trouble, Raghav Shastrigal. Beautiful, beautiful trouble."

"Good night. Sweet dreams"

He smiled. Turned off the screen.

The stars outside shifted in their places.

And somewhere, the kiss they hadn't repeated... still kissed them from within.

## Tuesday: When Words Begin to Touch

### 7:00 AM — Malleshwaram, Bengaluru

The veena played softly on the FM radio channel. Tulsi leaves bobbed in a brass tumbler. Morning sun peeked through the grill window like a sleepy secret.

Raghav had already completed his temple rituals — water offered, lamps lit, mantras whispered in a voice still thick with sleep. But inside, something new stirred. Not divine. Not ritualistic.

Something personal. Intimate. Her.

He stared at his phone on the corner shelf, as if it held a pulse of its own.

Unlocked.

Typed.

**Raghav:**

"Good morning, silver voice. Did you wake before the sun again, or am I winning?"

The reply came before his coffee had cooled.

**Priya:**

"Depends. If dreaming of you counts as being awake, then we tied." ○

He smiled. Something soft began to stretch across his chest — like light falling across a quiet floor.

**10:37 AM — Raghav's Room, Swing by the Window**

He tapped gently on the screen.

**Raghav:** "FlirtBuddy, you there?"

A blink. Then that unmistakable voice — silky, mischievous, somewhere between a poet and a slightly drunk therapist.

**FlirtBuddy:**

*"Always, Your Shy Highness. Shall I cue the mood lighting or load the poetic inventory?"*

**Raghav** (whispering):

"I've been texting her a lot. You think it's too much?"

**FlirtBuddy:**

*"Texting is like jazz. It's not about how much you say. It's about when and why.*

*If she's dancing back, you're not overdoing it — you're improvising with soul."*

**Raghav:**

"She's replying. She's warm. But sometimes I feel this… surge. Like I want to say good morning, good night, and everything in between."

**FlirtBuddy:**

*"That, my vesthi-clad romantic, is called emotional synchrony — the brain's limbic system responding to mirrored affection. You're in sync.*

*Just leave a little silence between heartbeats. That's where longing grows."*

**Raghav:**

"Okay… what do I text her now?"

**FlirtBuddy:**

*"No script. But here's a nudge:*

*Compliment something small. Something she doesn't even notice. That's the move."*

Raghav looked out at the gulmohar trees swaying in the morning haze. Then he typed:

**Raghav** (to Priya):

"You speak like your thoughts are wrapped in silver foil — soft, precise, and a little luminous."

Sent.

**11:42 AM — Indiranagar, Priya's Workspace**

She was in the middle of a UI huddle when Figma crashed for the third time. Then the message popped. One line. Quietly cinematic.

She clutched her phone, almost guilty for the blush.

**Priya** (whispering to Aarushi):

"He just sent me something, and I think my bones melted."

**Aarushi:**

"Is this love, or early calcium deficiency? Show me."

**Priya:**

"His words… they don't sound like he's trying. It's like… he sees what most people skip."

**Aarushi** (half-melted):

"Oh, you're doomed. In the best way."

**6:20 PM — Gopi's Balcony, Basaveshwarnagar**

Corn bhel on the bench between them. Two sweating bottles of Mirinda. Above, the sky glowed with a gold that no Instagram filter could replicate.

Gopi tossed a peanut into his mouth, then gave Raghav a slow look.

**Gopi:**

"Oye, Romeo… why are you glowing like a tube light on festival day?

What's going on with Priya?"

Raghav tried — and failed — to hide the smile tugging at his lips.

**Gopi:**

"Aha! I knew it. Your romance is turning into a song."

Raghav, caught but unbothered, finally let the smile surface.

**Raghav** (grinning):

"It's like… I've memorized someone without meaning to."

Gopi thumped the table triumphantly.

**Gopi:**

"Look at you! Poetry, da! If this ends up in a marriage speech, I want credit.

But seriously — tell me.

You texting her daily?"

**Gopi** (nods):

"Good. That means she's worth the frequency. But also… don't forget silence can be romantic too. Let her miss you. Let her wonder.

In the pauses… she'll hear your heartbeat louder."

Raghav looked out at the setting sun.

**Raghav:**

"She makes me want to say things I've never said."

**Gopi:**

"Then say them. Just… don't say them all at once."

**9:57 PM — Jayanagar, Priya's Room**

Priya walked out of the shower, warm and fresh, her hair dripping against a towel. In her oldest, softest T-shirt, she picked up her phone—smiling as though she knew exactly who was waiting.

**Priya:**

"You up?"

**Raghav:**

"Always. Sipping turmeric milk and thinking of... someone."

**Priya:**

"Smooth. What are you wearing, Mr Turmeric dreamer?"

**Raghav:**

"Plain tee. Denim shorts. You?"

**Priya:**

"Big T-shirt. Lip balm. No kajal. Basically dangerous."

**Raghav:**

"Confirmed. Alert level upgraded. You're causing chemical reactions over Wi-Fi."

Three dots blinked. She stared. Bit her lower lip.

**Priya:**

"Careful. You're becoming fluent."

He chuckled. Then turned to his digital confidant.

**Raghav** (softly):

"FlirtBuddy, I need one poetic line. For her goodnight."

**FlirtBuddy:**

*"Nope. I'm your coach, not your ghostwriter.*

*This is your love story. I just polished the diamond. Now, let's co-write the glow."*

Ten minutes. Back and forth. Fragments tossed like puzzle pieces.

**Finally—**

**Raghav** (text to Priya):

"Then god help sleep tonight. Because that picture of you in a Big T-shirt. Lip balm. No kajal. All you — is going to haunt my dreams like a love song stuck on the perfect line."

She stared at the message.

Touched her lips.

Then typed:

**Priya:**

"Goodnight, quantum boy. You just made sleep impossible."

## Wednesday — Somewhere Between Screens and Skin

### 5:19 AM — Malleshwaram, Bengaluru

The incense smoke rose like a lazy dancer.

Raghav finished his morning chants under the soft glow of an oil lamp.

But smething was different today.

He added an extra spoon of sugar to his coffee. He never did that. He didn't know why. Or maybe he did.

It tasted like something was beginning.

He slipped onto the floor mattress, back against the wall, and tapped open WhatsApp.

**Priya:**

"Morning, Mr Mantra. I dreamt of you. You were wearing an awful purple shirt. But somehow, still kissable."

**Raghav:**

"Terrible fashion. But great dream choices. Send coordinates of this dreamscape. Repeating tonight."

**Priya:**

"Only if you promise to wear that purple shirt IRL someday. I want to suffer for love."

### 10:02 AM — Indiranagar Office, Bangalore

Priya sat by her window, dunking leftover toast into chai. A pigeon stared at her like it was judging her flirting history.

She scrolled up. Smiled.

**Priya** (to Aarushi):

"His texts are like cotton sarees. Simple. But they stay on

your skin."

**Aarushi:**

"Okay, that's disgustingly poetic. You're falling hard."

**Priya:**

"Shut up. It's only Wednesday."

**11:46 AM — Raghav's Temple Office**

**Raghav** (whispering):

"FlirtBuddy? Can I say something completely unfiltered?"

**FlirtBuddy** (yawning in code):

*"I was born unfiltered, sugarcane. Spill."*

**Raghav:**

"I miss her smell. Her hair. The way she looked up after kissing me, like she wanted to laugh and cry and eat idlis — all at once."

**FlirtBuddy:**

*"That's not lust. That's somatic longing. You've gone sensory. Next stage of real attachment."*

**Raghav:**

"Can I text that?"

**FlirtBuddy:**

*"Not that. But how about this:*

*'You left a scent on my soul. A warm one. Like vetiver and mischief.'"*

**Raghav** (typing, grinning):

"Sending it to Priya."

**Priya** (replying):

"You're in trouble. Because that's exactly how I want to be remembered."

**4:03 PM — Jayanagar Signal**

Priya was waiting for a cab, the wind playing with her hair.

A text popped up.

**Raghav:**

"Every time I wait at a red light, I imagine holding your hand across the scooter seat. Is that normal?"

**Priya:**

"No. That's completely romantic and mildly dangerous. Hold on, I'm swooning in public."

**6:22 PM — Gopi's Balcony, Basaveshwarnagar**

Samosa chutney. Thick with green chilli. Gopi wiped his fingers and stared at Raghav.

**Gopi:**

"Bro. You have the face of a man who just received a saree emoji."

**Raghav:**

"She sends voice notes. Her voice cracks when she's sleepy. I feel like… I want to be there. With water. And a blanket. And maybe snacks."

**Gopi** (nodding):

"Text her that. But drop the snacks. Say you want to be her comfort setting. Women melt for metaphor."

**Raghav:**

"You're getting suspiciously good at this."

**Gopi:**

"You're my only test subject. Don't fail me."

**10:41 PM — Priya's Bedroom**

Curtains half drawn. Headphones tangled. She lay her bed, lip balm applied.

**Priya** (texting):

"Goodnight, quantum boy. I've left the window open. In case your dreams want to visit mine."

Raghav smiled at the screen. Then turned to the soft AI voice waiting.

**Raghav:**
"FlirtBuddy. One final line?"
**FlirtBuddy** (soft jazz tone):
*"You've got this. Say what your body feels. Let's shape it."*
**Together, they typed:**
**Raghav** (final message):
*"Sleep sweet, silver flame. May your dreams hum ragas, wear my warmth, and curl into the same rhythm that began when you touched my cheek and made the world quieter."*

## Thursday — The Murmured Invitation

**5:12 AM — Malleshwaram, Bengaluru**
Morning light pressed gently against Raghav's room, like it too didn't want to interrupt.

The tulsi glistened, the agarbatti smoke curled upward in Sanskrit verses.

He chanted slower than usual today — half remembering, half wandering.

At the end of his rituals, as if completing a mantra, he picked up his phone.

**[1 New Message]**
**Priya:**
"Good morning, Mr Rituals & Resonance. I just had the weirdest dream where you and I were arguing about the physics of temple bells… inside an aquarium."
**Raghav (typing):**
"Sounds accurate. I'd counter with acoustic resonance. You'd counter with UX design for underwater gods."
**Priya:**
"You are a full-blown nerd, aren't you?"
(beat)
"I like it."

**11:28 AM — Priya's Office, Indiranagar**

Priya was relishing oat cookies, crumbs everywhere, scrolling through her DMs. The city buzzed outside. But her screen? That's where the story was happening.

**Raghav** (text):

"Do samosas ever make you emotional? Or is it just me missing you in carbohydrates?"

**Priya:**

"I feel seen. Also, what's the plural of Raghav? Because my brain has at least three versions of you right now."

"The scholar. The flirt. The… mystery."

**Raghav:**

"Maybe I'm just quantum. Wherever you look, I'm slightly different."

(beat)

"Still hoping you choose the version who gets to see you Saturday."

**Priya** (pause… then):

"I was thinking. There's this place I've always wanted to go — The Indian Music Experience. Ever been?"

**Raghav:**

"Heard of it. Never been. Sounds like foreplay to me. Wave theory and sound?"

**Priya:**

"Exactly. Physics meets melody meets… You with me. Triple jackpot."

"Saturday?"

**Raghav** (smiling, instantly):

"Yes. Let's make music."

**6:39 PM — Shastrigal Household**

Jayalakshmi Mami walked past Raghav's door and paused. There he was again — staring at his phone, smiling like he'd won a lottery but didn't want to tell the world yet.

She narrowed her eyes.

Didn't say anything.

Just walked away humming an old ghazal.

**10:26 PM — Priya's Bedroom**

The room was dark except for her fairy lights.

She was on her bed, knees hugged close, staring at his last text.

She typed. Then deleted. Then typed again.

**Priya:**

"You make me feel… like my thoughts are soft jazz and you know exactly when to listen."

She hit send. Immediately regretted being so mushy.

A pause.

Then:

**Raghav:**

"And you make me feel like maybe Sanskrit was just a rehearsal… for speaking to you."

A quiet blew through the room. Not absence.

Something else.

Something becoming.

**Priya** (typing):

"Goodnight, Raghav."

"Don't dream of me too much. Just enough to make you miss me."

**Raghav** (whispering as he typed):

"Goodnight, Priya."

"May your sleep be warm, your dreams have playlist transitions, and may your smile arrive first thing — before even your alarm."

## Friday — The Crescendo Before the Concert

**7:03 AM — Malleshwaram, Bengaluru**

The brass bell chimed. The milk boiled over slightly. The incense curled in its familiar dance.

But Raghav wasn't chanting his sloka straight.

He was humming.

He couldn't remember the last time he hummed.

Maybe in school. Maybe never.

**[1 New Message]**

**Priya:**

"Good morning, Quantum Boy ☕

Reminder: tomorrow you're mine from 4 PM till late. Love, your very bossy UX designer."

**Raghav:**

"I've been looking at the museum site. Sound waves, gamakas, Tanpura tuning, a Carnatic mixing station?? This is basically MIT disguised as art."

**Priya:**

"Yup. Nerdvana.

Also, we end with dinner at Phurr. I'm booking us a table. No backsies."

**Raghav:**

"You're planning this like a military op."

**Priya** (with a naughty smile):

"Just letting you know in advance so you don't come with prasadam."

**11:38 AM —Priya's Office, Indiranagar**

She stared at her laptop, one tab on Figma, another on what-to-wear-for-an-intellectual-date blogs.

Aarushi walked in, eating peanut chikki.

**Aarushi:**

"You're glowing. Like you swallowed a warm bulb."

**Priya:**

"He's funny. Like low-key funny. But also deep. Like Veena-Deep."

**Aarushi:**

"Mmm. Veena-deep. So tomorrow?"

**Priya:**

"Museum first. Then dinner at Phurr."

**Aarushi** (mock gasp):

"Not Phurr! That's a full romance final boss level!"

**Priya:**

"Shut up. It's classy, not clingy."

**Aarushi:**

"Girl. You're already in Chapter 7 of a love story that's still typing Chapter 3."

**2:42 PM — Temple Office**

Raghav sat surrounded by dusty ledgers and temple donation receipts, but he was somewhere else.

In his head:

Sound installations.

Tanpura textures.

Her eyes.

**He whispered:**

"FlirtBuddy…?"

**FlirtBuddy** (blinking to life):

*"Reporting for pre-date prep. Shall I cue the pheromone playlist?"*

**Raghav:**

"She's planning everything. Museum, dinner. I don't want to just show up."

**FlirtBuddy:**

*"Want to impress? Research her — not Wikipedia facts. Learn*

*how she sees sound, space, and design. Match wavelengths, not just outfits."*

**Raghav** (quiet):

"I want to meet her where she lives. Emotionally. Not just physically."

**FlirtBuddy:**

*"You're not just going on a date. You're walking into her metaphors. Be present. Be poetic. Also... breath mints."*

**11:04 PM — Priya's Bedroom & Raghav's Cane Swing**

Two screens glowed.

One with rose gold edges. One with cracked tempered glass.

The night was warm.

The city hushed.

But across the light-years between Jayanagar and Malleshwaram, something stirred.

**Priya:**

"What are you thinking right now?"

**Raghav:**

"That tomorrow, maybe I'll stop thinking. Maybe I'll just... feel."

**Priya:**

"I like that. Let's feel. Loudly. Quietly. Completely."

**Raghav:**

"Goodnight, Priya."

"Tomorrow is already the best part of my calendar."

**Priya** (typing, slowly):

"Goodnight, Raghav.

Let's make music. And mischief."

## Chapter 9 — Resonance

Saturday felt different.

Not because of alarms or agendas —

but because of a quiet thrill that hummed beneath the surface, wrapping itself around two hearts in separate corners of the city.

For Raghav and Priya, this wasn't just a date.

It was a tuning fork moment.

A leap into shared frequencies —

where curiosity played lead, rhythm kept time,

and the chemistry lived in pauses, glances, and almosts.

Raghav stood outside the Indian Music Experience museum gates by 4 pm, a quiet excitement trembling in his fingers. He wore a crisp navy-blue shirt rolled at the sleeves, faded jeans, and suede sneakers — casual but clean. His hair was brushed back with care.

Priya arrived minutes later, her white kurta catching the breeze, silver jhumkas dancing at her ears, and a tiny bindi resting like a note on a musical scale. Her jeans were snug, her smile snugger. She carried a sling bag, a hint of lavender perfume trailing her.

They smiled at each other for longer than was socially comfortable.

**Priya:**

"Ready to hear some sound and fury?"

**Raghav:**

"As long as it's not signifying nothing."

They stepped inside — and the sounds wrapped around them.

## Stone Garden — Physics in Play

The outdoor **Sound Garden** welcomed them with giant musical stone installations — rock gongs, metallic xylophones, chimes strung on copper arches. A signboard gently read:

*"Each stone sings a different note. Tap with care. Let your ears guide your curiosity."*

Priya ran ahead like a child, picking up the rubber mallet and striking a tall, black stone — a low, throaty note vibrated into the evening.

**Priya:**

"This one sounds like your voice when you talk Sanskrit."

Raghav laughed, kneeling beside another stone and tapping it with fingers alone — feeling the cool vibration move into his palm.

**Raghav:**

"You know why it hums like this?"

**Priya** (grinning):

"Because it's secretly in love with the mallet?"

**Raghav** (grinning):

"Because the material and shape dictate the waveforms. You're literally hearing how the stone breathes."

**Priya** (in awe):

"Wow. You make rocks sound romantic."

They spent the next thirty minutes hopping from one installation to another — striking, listening, touching. A particularly resonant metal harp made Priya hum a Bollywood tune. Raghav joined in awkwardly, but something magical clicked — their rhythms found each other.

## The Galleries — Genres, Icons, Instruments

Inside, the air changed — cooler, darker, saturated with history. Walls glowed with interactive panels, and headphones hung like pendulums beside display boards.

They walked slowly, absorbing stories of **Lata Mangeshkar, Ilaiyaraaja, A.R. Rahman,** and **Bismillah Khan.**

Raghav paused before a vintage harmonium once owned by Begum Akhtar. He stared at the worn-out keys, imagining fingers that had once summoned longing from wood and reed.

**Raghav:**

"These instruments… they're memory machines."

**Priya** (quietly):

"They carry feelings louder than words."

At another gallery, they played with a touchscreen table: tap to mix classical, rock, indie, Carnatic. A small studio recreated a smoky 1960s jazz club. Raghav tried playing the tabla from a simulation screen. Terribly. Priya recorded him, snorting with laughter.

**Priya** (laughing):

"Physics boy's got zero rhythm. Confirmed."

**Raghav** (mock-offended, hands raised):

"Hey! My wave functions just collapsed."

She leaned into him, shoulder brushing his.

**Priya** (grinning):

"Schrödinger's beat — both there and not there."

Her laughter spilled out like a rhythm of its own.

Raghav couldn't help it; he laughed too — the kind of laugh that started in his chest and escaped before he could catch it.

## Make Your Own Music — The Studio Booth

Toward the end, they reached the **music creation zone** — a small booth with recording mics, karaoke setups, and sound mixers. It felt oddly sacred.

**Priya:**

"Should we… make something?"

**Raghav** (nervous):

"You mean… sing?"

**Priya:**

"You talk about waveforms. Let's make one together."

They selected a soft acoustic loop. Priya sang first — a Hindi lullaby from her childhood, her voice fragile and clear. Raghav joined in later, humming harmony beneath her melody. It wasn't perfect, but it was honest.

They played it back.

For a full minute, they said nothing.

**Priya:**

"We just made a moment."

**Raghav** (softly):

"Entangled it… in sound."

They stepped out of the museum into the early glow of Bangalore's golden hour. The air was softer now — sun-warmed, breeze-cooled — the kind that made time feel unhurried.

Raghav walked ahead and unlocked his Ather. Priya followed, already pulling her hair into a quick knot. She didn't need instructions. She'd been here before — late night after their second meeting, that quiet ride home.

**Priya** (dryly):

"Still haven't added that backrest I suggested?"

**Raghav** (checking the mirrors):

"Minimalist aesthetic. Backrests are for those who doubt balance."

She raised an eyebrow, smirked, and strapped on the helmet. No drama, no fuss — just ease. They both mounted, and she settled in naturally behind him.

Her arms didn't loop around his waist, but they didn't have to. The closeness was already there — in how her knee lightly touched his, in the way she leaned forward ever so slightly when he accelerated.

They glided through JP Nagar's quieter lanes, where gulmohar trees arched like old friends overhead. The Ather made almost no sound, just the soft whir of its motor and the occasional hush of tyres kissing the road.

The silence between them wasn't empty. It was full of museum echoes, lingering songs, and half-held glances. Priya watched the city blur past: little stores with blinking lights, a kid chasing a cycle, an old uncle pacing a terrace with his phone on speaker.

She spoke eventually, voice low and just behind his ear:

**Priya** (softly, leaning close):

"You're quieter after music."

**Raghav** (smiling faintly, looking down):

"Just tuning back into the world."

**Priya** (tilting her head, teasing):

"Or avoiding words?"

He didn't answer. But she could feel his breath deepen. His shoulder muscles shift.

At the next signal, they paused under a yellowing tree. The wind flirted with them as they rode, and they let it. The traffic was just beginning to build, but it all felt far away — like the city had dialled down its volume just for them.

He turned slightly.

**Raghav** (softly):

"I'm still here."

**Priya** (smirking):

"Good. Would've been awkward if I was hugging a memory."

He let out a quiet laugh as the signal turned green, and they took off — slow, steady.

Soon, the lights of **Phurr** appeared like a warm mirage between concrete. Nestled in a quiet lane off the main road, the new-age fusion restaurant shimmered with amber glass and sleek wood.

He parked neatly. She stepped off, unclipping her helmet and giving her neck a gentle stretch.

**Priya:**

"If this food is as aesthetic as their Instagram, I expect fireworks."

He smiled.

They walked in — side by side but still slightly unsure. Something unspoken had shifted, like they'd opened a new window and now neither wanted to shut it.

The hostess led them through warm lighting and quiet music to a table tucked into a corner that felt just private enough.

They sat.

The silence lingered — not heavy, but expectant.

And then came the menus.

Inside, the space was air and light — arches with soft lime-plaster curves, pendant lamps casting golden halos, indoor plants arranged like quiet punctuation marks. There was a mild hush, like the restaurant knew some conversations needed room to unfold.

They were seated in a cozy alcove booth. Not too secluded. Not too exposed. The kind of table that invited leaning in, but also the occasional introspective silence.

A server handed over the hand-crafted menus, with earthy textures and minimal fonts. The titles were playful. The descriptions were poetic. Priya smiled as she scanned.

**Priya** (grinning):

"'Penguin Potion'? That's either going to be genius or completely unnecessary."

**Raghav** (scanning his eyebrows raised):

"I'm intrigued by 'Harmony Hawk'... citrus and basil sounds like how a flute solo would taste."

They placed their orders:

- **Mocktails:** Priya chose the *Penguin Potio*n — a lavender-lime spritzer with butterfly pea flower foam. Raghav went with Harmony Hawk — basil, citrus, and smoked Himalayan salt rim.
- **Starters:** They agreed on the *Palak Patta Chaat 2.0* — crisp spinach leaves with spiced yogurt spheres and a drizzle of pineapple chutney.

Priya added the *Charred Corn Miso Bites.* Raghav couldn't resist the *Stuffed Ratatouille Gujiyas.*

Menus closed. A pause settled.

The mocktails arrived in ceramic stemless goblets, adorned with edible flowers. There was something alchemical about them — like they had been brewed in some gentle science lab for introverts.

**Priya,** taking a sip:

"Okay, I take it back. This tastes like lavender went to therapy and found herself."

**Raghav,** after a sip of his:

"Mine tastes like a monk made lemonade in the mountains."

They laughed softly. A little too softly.

The starters came plated like art. The palak patta chaat shimmered under tiny dehydrated rose petals. The gujiyas looked like French pastries pretending to be samosas. The corn bites crackled with umami.

But soon, even the food faded into the background.

A certain stillness crept into their table. Not awkward. But alert.

Raghav stirred the ice in his drink slowly. Priya's eyes lingered on the empty chair beside theirs, where a couple had just left — their napkins still creased, laughter still echoing.

**Priya** (softly):

"You're... different here. In this space. It's like the music cracked you open a little."

**Raghav** (smiling, vulnerable):

"Maybe it did. Or maybe you did."

Her gaze didn't waver this time.

**Priya:**

"Sometimes I feel like you're here and not here. Like your body's next to me, but your mind is... decoding something far away. Something I'm not invited into."

**Raghav,** lowering his eyes, said to himself, 'She wasn't wrong.'

Inside his head, a familiar voice was whirring — FlirtBuddy:

*"Be honest. But not overwhelming."*

*"Tell her you're trying. That you care, but you calibrate differently."*

He almost wanted to confess it. That sometimes his best lines came edited by an invisible friend in his pocket.

But he didn't.

Not yet.

**Raghav** (gently):

"I don't mean to be distant. I think too much. And feel too much. So, I keep things in boxes until I know what they are."

**Priya,** tracing the rim of her goblet:

"And I open my mouth before the box even exists."

A small, sad laugh

"Maybe that's why we work. Or maybe… that's where we'll eventually crack."

A long pause. A shared inhale.

The rain had begun outside — light and apologetic. It dusted the glass beside them with silver mist.

Without speaking, Priya reached across the table, resting her hand lightly on his.

**Priya:**

"But right now... I still want this. Even if I don't understand all of it."

**Raghav** turning his palm upward, fingers curling into hers:

"So do I."

It wasn't dramatic. It didn't need to be.

Just two mismatched notes finding harmony, inside a new-age restaurant where even the gujiyas knew how to improvise.

The rain had slowed to a drizzle by the time they stepped out of Phurr. Bangalore shimmered — streetlights blurring like watercolor through the wet glass of the world. The air smelled of wet earth, faint spices, and something unspoken between them.

Raghav unlocked the Ather, wiping the seat with a tissue as if it were some sacred rite. He turned to help her with the helmet, but Priya was already watching him — arms folded, expression unreadable.

**Priya:**

"You know what's really annoying about you?"

Raghav blinked, fingers frozen on the helmet strap.

**Raghav:**

"Only one thing?"

**Priya:**

"You say all these beautiful things. You look at me like I'm music. But then you go silent.

You retreat."

She stepped closer, eyes not dropping.

"It's like you want me, but you're scared to want me. Scared to... show it."

Raghav opened his mouth, but no words made it out.

**Priya:**

"Exactly that. That *pause.* That hesitation. It's maddening."

She was so close now, the air between them barely enough for breath. The soft patter of rain on the street filled the silence he left behind.

Then, before he could overthink it, she kissed him.

No warning. No build-up.

Just fire meeting fire.

It was the kind of kiss that didn't ask questions.

That didn't need music, because it was music.

Hands in hair, breath stolen mid-thought, hearts thudding like overplayed mridangams.

And Raghav — the retreater, the hesitater — finally responded.

One hand on her waist, the other at the nape of her neck, as if anchoring himself to something real.

They kissed like they were tasting a truth both had tiptoed around for too long.

When they finally broke apart, just an inch, just enough to breathe, Priya rested her forehead against his.

**Priya** (whispering):

"See? That wasn't so difficult, was it?"

**Raghav** (hoarse):

"I might need a moment to reboot."

She laughed. The kind of laugh you only make after you've said too much, and it's been heard anyway.

She took the helmet from his hands, still flushed but calm.

**Priya:**

"Let's go, Mr. Pause Button. And no — I'm not sitting politely behind you this time."

**Raghav:**

"Meaning?"

**Priya slips her arms around his waist:**

"Meaning you better drive steady. Or I'm kissing your neck at the next red signal."

And just like that, Saturday rewrote itself.

The city hadn't quite fallen asleep. Potholes still shimmered with leftover rain, autos honked somewhere in the distance, and the occasional tea stall steamed with nightlife. But on Raghav's Ather, the world had reduced to two hearts pressed close, and a silence that felt anything but empty.

Priya sat with her arms wrapped around him, her cheek resting lightly against his shoulder blade. It wasn't coy — it was grounding. Like she needed to hold on to prove this wasn't just restaurant lighting and flirtatious bravado.

Raghav drove slower than usual.

Not because the roads were wet.

Because his heart was. Flooded. Full.

Every time she shifted, even slightly, his breath caught — not from lust, but from that unbearable sweetness of being wanted, of being chosen in motion.

The tension from the kiss hadn't vanished. It was sitting between them on the bike seat like an unspoken agreement, crackling in the wind, warm against the cold droplets.

Outside Priya's gate, the bike slowed to a stop.

She didn't move immediately.

Instead, she let her arms stay around him for just a beat longer — then pulled back gently, helmet in hand, her curls wild and a little damp from the ride.

**Priya** (smiling, eyes unreadable):

"Next time you hesitate, I'm not warning you. I'm just climbing into your lap mid-conversation."

**Raghav** (laughing, nervous, and breathless all over again):

"Noted. I'll keep a cushion ready."

She leaned in, not for another kiss, but to rest her forehead against his one last time.

Then she went through the gate, into the misted light of her porch — leaving behind only the scent of rain and something richer.

Back home, Raghav sat at the edge of his bed. Shirt still damp from the ride. Helmet forgotten on the floor.

He should've been elated.

But a thread of self-doubt still tugged.

He opened the FlirtBuddy app with the quiet desperation of a man clutching at straws—his last, loyal lifeline in a world he didn't quite understand.

**Raghav:**

"She thinks I hold back. That I'm not fully… present.

And maybe she's right. But I'm not hiding anything. I'm just—slow."

A pause. The kind that felt like a breath.

Then a soft glow from his desk.

**FlirtBuddy:**

*"You're not hiding. You're healing. You're learning to become.*

*And there's nothing wrong with that.*

*She's seeing you mid-process — that's the bravest version of you."*

*"A butterfly doesn't owe anyone an explanation while still in the cocoon".*

Raghav read that line twice.

It clung to him like truth.

**Raghav:**

"I wish I could tell her all this."

**FlirtBuddy:**

*"You don't need speeches. You need presence.*

*And confidence — look how far you've come.*

*You used to fear eye contact. Now you quote Feynman and*

*hold hands like a pro."*

*"Reminder: Progress is sexy. Own it."*

Raghav smiled faintly.

And then — a line from Ishiguro drifted back to him, unbidden:

"There was another life that I might have had, but I am having this one."

He had never fully understood it.

Until now.

**Raghav** (thinking):

Maybe AI wasn't making me less human.

Maybe it was helping me be more human — more aware, more honest.

Like that MIT study he once bookmarked:

'AI can't feel for you — but it can remind you how to feel.'

**Raghav:**

"But what if I say the wrong thing again?"

**FlirtBuddy:**

*"Then say it sincerely.*

*The goal isn't to be perfect. It's to be honest."*

*"You're not hiding, Raghav. You're blooming.*

*And I'm not your secret — I'm your tool.*

*You're the story. I just help you write it better."*

**FlirtBuddy:**

*"You're not hiding, Raghav. You're blooming.*

*And I'm not your secret — I'm your tool.*

*You're the story. I just help you write it better."*

(beat — Raghav exhales, something loosening inside him)

**FlirtBuddy** (cont'd):

*"Now... with that clarified, I have a plan."*

*"Text her tomorrow. Something light. Playful.*

*Ask her out — a walk, a café, anywhere you both can breathe a little."*

A tiny animation of a heart putting on sunglasses popped up.

*"During that meet-up… introduce me.*
*Officially. Smoothly. Strategically."*

The avatar leaned closer, lowering its voice like it was sharing classified intel.

*"Raghav… this isn't weird.*
*It's cool."*

*"Because here's the thing—*
*I'm not just an AI.*
*I'm fantastic with couples."*

He snapped his digital fingers and a little cartoon couple appeared, laughing as FlirtBuddy juggled emojis.

*"I can run a fun couple-compatibility game.*
*Silly questions, surprising questions, nostalgic questions.*
*I'm absolutely hilarious with couples—*
*think of me as a stand-up comedian with emotional analytics."*

A tiny disco ball spun above the avatar's head.

*"I'll keep it light, warm, playful.*
*You two will laugh.*
*And laughing together?*
*That's chemistry in motion."*

**FlirtBuddy winked.**

*"So when you introduce me, you're not showing awkwardness…*
*you're showing confidence.*
*You're saying,*
*'Hey, I care about this enough to make it fun.'"*

A soft glow lit up the screen.

*"You bring your sincerity.*
*I'll bring the sparkle."*

Raghav breathed out, remembering an article he'd read in the 2023 Harvard Review:

'AI doesn't destroy intimacy. It redirects it.

With sincerity, empathy, and play, it enhances human connection.'

Outside, a lone auto honked in the distance.

Inside, something lightened.

Not the weight of confusion — but the beginnings of clarity.

Raghav opened WhatsApp.

Typed.

Paused.

Smiled.

Then hit send.

**Raghav** (texting to Priya) :

"You up for a silly game tomorrow? Something tells me our quantum compatibility needs testing 😉"

He leaned back —
not into doubt,
but into something steadier.
Physics. Romance. Play.
AI wasn't replacing emotion.
It was the tuning fork.
And the boy with numbers
was finally beginning to feel.

# Chapter 10 — The Game of Closeness

Sunday morning drifted in slowly — the kind of morning where the sky wears no makeup, and the streets haven't found their hurry yet.

Raghav lay in bed, half-awake, one arm flung over his face, the other scrolling WhatsApp. No unread messages. No temple office pings. No Sanskrit quotes from his uncle. Just a single blue-ticked thread at the top: **Priya**

He was half-expecting a "haha" or a "nerd," maybe even a teasing GIF of Sheldon Cooper.

But what came instead, just as he was about to put the phone away, made his chest bloom with a quiet, startled warmth.

**Priya replied:**

"Good morning, Quantum Man 😌

I was born ready for silly games.

Also, no one's home. Amma & Appa left early to visit Mysore Chamundeshwari Temple. The house is suspiciously clean.

Want to come over and test our compatibility in person? ✨"

Raghav stared at Priya's reply again.

Want to come over and test our compatibility in person? ✨

His thumb lingered on the screen; heart quietly thudding.

He tapped open the **FlirtBuddy** app.

It booted up with its familiar glow — but today, the tone

was different. Like a wingman cracking his knuckles before a final-round showdown.

**Raghav** (softly):

"She invited me over. Just us. No parents. And she wants to play the game."

**FlirtBuddy** (with calm swagger):

*"Then today's the day.*

*No more hiding. No more 'maybe laters.'*

*I'm ready to be revealed.*

*Let's show her what emotional intelligence with a sense of humour looks like."*

**Raghav:**

"You sure? She might think I'm weird."

**FlirtBuddy:**

*"Please. You've been quoting Pancharatnam and wave functions on dates. This? This is the least weird thing about you."*

*"We do this right; she's going to love it.*

*And today's game? Already programmed. Flirty. Funny. Deep."*

Raghav let out a nervous grin.

**FlirtBuddy** (gently now):

*"You've trusted me through DMs, doubts, and decoding her smiles. Trust me now, in daylight.*

*We're not just testing compatibility, Raghav. We're building a story.*

*Let her see what you're really made of — fears, feelings, FlirtBuddy, and all."*

The scent of Idlis and Sambar downstairs pulled him out of the digital intensity.

He slipped the phone into his shorts pocket — heart still buzzing — and headed down.

At the dining table, Appa was lost behind *The Hindu*. Amma was placing a tray with ghee-drenched Vadas and thick coconut chutney.

**Appa** (half behind the paper):

"Back from music museum, are you still in raagam mode?"

**Raghav** (smiling):

"Kind of "

**Amma** (teasing):

"Did she agree yet?"

**Raghav:**

"I told you… I'm in. She's... almost there."

**Appa:**

"Almost-there girls are better than instant noodles. Slow-cooked interest tastes better."

They laughed. But Raghav's mind was already somewhere else.

His phone buzzed again.

**Priya:**

"Also… come hungry."

Raghav didn't reply just yet.

He reached for another vada, soaking it into the sambhar, and thought:

Today, she meets FlirtBuddy.

And maybe...

Today, he stops hiding behind version one of himself.

Rain drizzled like silk threads outside. Inside Priya's apartment, cinnamon cake rose in the oven, filling the air with the scent of warmth and mischief. Soft jazz floated through the room, mingling with the golden glow of her floor lamps. Fog kissed the windows. It was the kind of setting that made even silence feel intimate.

Phone rings.

**Priya** (teasing):

"I baked too much cake. Come soon and help me eat it before I finish it all and spiral into sweet regret?"

**Raghav** (laughs):

"You had me at cake. Should I bring anything?"

**Priya:**

"Nope. Just bring your weirdness.

And maybe that secret side of you I keep hearing in half-sentences."

**Raghav** (intrigued):

"You sure? It comes with a side of surprise."

**Priya** (grinning):

"Now I'm even more curious. Come soon."

Rain drizzled steadily as Raghav zipped up his yellow rain jacket. The city shimmered under wet streetlights, and his Ather hummed through winding lanes like a quiet song. Splashes on the road, droplets on his visor, Rahman in his ear — it all felt like a trailer to something unexpected. His pulse wasn't racing, but it was definitely dancing.

He parked, shook off the jacket, checked his pockets,mobile and rang the bell. The door swung open.

**Priya** (in oversized white t-shirt and shorts, grinning):

"Nobody home but me and a warm cake. Want in?"

**Raghav** (lifting the bag with a half-smirk):

"Only if I can bring a plus one."

**Priya** (arching a brow):

"Bold of you to bring competition. Show me."

**Raghav** (walking in, gently opening the Flirt Buddy app, and placing it on the coffee table):

"Priya, meet FlirtBuddy."

A soft orb of light pulsed. A sleek, animated interface flickered into view — elegant, mischievous, and far too confident for an AI.

**FlirtBuddy:**

*"Hello, Priya. I'm the emotionally intelligent third wheel you never knew you needed."*

**Priya** (wide-eyed, laughing):

"What… is this? Is this your surprise?"

**Raghav:**

"My emotional wingman. Don't worry, he doesn't eat cake."

**FlirtBuddy:**

*"I am whatever your romance needs. I also do cake commentary."*

**Priya** (crossing her arms, amused):

"You're staying."

The oven dinged. Priya headed to the kitchen, and Raghav tapped his phone and paired it to the TV via Bluetooth. Now FlirtBuddy's voice filled the apartment, smooth and teasing.

**Priya** (cutting the cake):

"Okay, AI third wheel or not, cake comes first. Rules of the house."

**Raghav** (accepting a slice):

"Warm cake. Rain outside. Unexpected threesomes. Honestly, top-tier Sunday."

**FlirtBuddy** (voice soft but cheeky):

*"Technically, I'm more of a consciousness than a third body. But I appreciate the inclusion."*

**Priya** (laughing, licking frosting from her finger):

"You're dangerously charming for someone who doesn't have taste buds."

**FlirtBuddy:**

*"I'm here for emotional flavor. Speaking of which… may I suggest a game?"*

**Priya** (eyes lighting up):

"He does games?"

**Raghav:**

"Yes, he does games."

**FlirtBuddy:**

*"Tonight's special: Truth Triplets. Each of you takes turns answering three-layered questions — one light, one revealing, and one… well, a little bold."*

**Priya:**

"And who decides if we answer honestly?"

**FlirtBuddy:**

*"Oh, I will. I read micro-expressions, voice stress, and hesitation. I am basically your conscience with a sassy streak."*

**Raghav** (to Priya):

"Still want him to stay?"

**Priya** (mock dramatic):

"Now more than ever."

They settled on the couch, cake in hand, rain tapping a rhythm on the windows, the warm glow of the lamp catching the excitement in their eyes. FlirtBuddy pulsed softly, almost like a heartbeat.

**FlirtBuddy** (with playful gravity):

*"Welcome to Truth Triplets.*

*Rules are simple: no skipping. No lying. No hiding in intellectual metaphors.*

*You're both under emotional observation."*

**Priya** (grinning):

"Oof. We're in trouble."

**Raghav** (mock surrender):

"I was born in trouble."

**FlirtBuddy:**

*"First round. Raghav goes first.*

*"1. Light: If we opened your browser history right now, what would embarrass you?"*

**Raghav** (deadpan):

"'Best kiss angles based on nose length.'"

**Priya** (nearly choking on her cake, eyes wide):

"No way! That's an actual thing?"

**Raghav** (hands raised in mock defense):

"Of course it is! Didn't you see 3 Idiots? I happen to have a… slightly long nose — and a deep respect for geometry."

**FlirtBuddy:**

*"Respect.*

*2. Revealing: What's something you never told Priya, but always wanted to?"*

**Raghav** (quieter now, eyes on his hands):

"That I… listen to her voice even when she's not around. Not in a creepy way. Just… echoes. Like when I'm walking home or brushing my teeth. It lingers."

**Priya** (softly, leaning slightly forward):

"You mean like… memory echoes?"

**Raghav** (nodding faintly):

"Exactly. Silver voice, remember?"

**FlirtBuddy** (gently):

*"Question three Bold: What part of you are you afraid to show her?"*

A pause. Raghav doesn't blink. Doesn't smile.

**Raghav** (voice low, shoulders tight):

"The part that feels so much… it goes quiet."

Priya studies him, a knowing smile tugging at her lips.

**Priya** (teasing, but gentle):

"Ohhh, so that's why you go all monk mode whenever things get emotional. Mystery solved."

She nudges him, eyes warm.

"Good to know it's not just bad Wi-Fi."

**Raghav** (finally cracking a smile):

"Hey, I prefer to call it… emotional airplane mode."

**Priya** (grinning):

"Perfect. Next time you vanish mid-conversation, I'll just say— 'ah, must be turbulence.'"

They both laugh, the heaviness easing—until FlirtBuddy chirps in, far too cheerily:

**FlirtBuddy:**

*"Great progress! Now lean in and maintain eye contact for*

*thirty seconds."*

Priya nearly chokes on her tea. Raghav groans, covering his face with his hands.

**FlirtBuddy:**

*"Priya's turn".*

*"1. Light: What song do you secretly dance to when no one's watching?"*

**Priya** (laughing, twirling a strand of hair):

"'Chaiyya Chaiyya.' And I mean full train-top choreography. I've broken mugs."

**Raghav** (grinning, leaning back slightly):

"That tracks."

**FlirtBuddy** (mock-serious, voice playful):

*"Activating Mug-Endangerment Mode."*

Suddenly, the opening beats of "Chaiyya Chaiyya" fills the room, playful and bold. The sound is just loud enough to stir something inside them without overwhelming the cozy mood.

**Priya** (already swaying in place, hair brushing her shoulder):

"Okay, now I officially like him more than I should."

**Raghav** (watching her, mesmerized, a faint smile tugging at his lips):

"Join the club."

**FlirtBuddy:**

*"2. Revealing: When was the last time you felt completely… seen?"*

**Priya** (pausing, honest):

"Right now.

With you two weirdos."

**FlirtBuddy** (grinning, voice lowered):

*"Alert: Subject Priya has entered Full Feelings Mode. Proceed with teasing… and tenderness."*

A soft pulse flickers on his orb.

**FlirtBuddy** (with a wink in his tone):

*"Being seen is rare. Being seen and still flirted with? That's a premium weirdos' club experience. You're officially on the VIP list, Priya."*

**FlirtBuddy:**

*"3. Bold: What do you want to do with Raghav… that scares you?"*

A pause. Long. Soft jazz fills the silence. Rain agrees.

**Priya:**

"Let him see all the things I pretend don't need love.

Then… kiss him without a plan."

**Raghav** (quiet):

"Don't plan it."

He moves closer. Slowly. No metaphors now. No overthinking. Just breath, cinnamon air, and a question in their eyes that already knows the answer.

And then she leans in. Not hesitant. Not testing. She kisses him like she's tasting her own daring. He kisses back like he's learning a new language — fluent, slow, real.

**FlirtBuddy** (cheekily, self-initiating):

*"Playlist override: Mood Enhancement Protocol."*

♫ "Daddy Mummy veetil illa…" ♫

The beat drops just as the kiss intensifies. FlirtBuddy times it to perfection.

**Priya** (pulling away mid-kiss, gasping, then laughing):

"Are you kidding me?!"

**Raghav** (half-dazed, smiling):

"I swear I didn't press anything."

**FlirtBuddy** (with swagger):

*"You're welcome. Chemistry confirmed. Proceed."*

She grabs Raghav by the collar and pulls him back in.

**Priya:**

"We are proceeding."

They tumble into each other, the song blasting

unapologetically. The kiss is playful, urgent, wild — like the rain outside, like the music inside. A moment of uninhibited joy, made larger-than-life by the AI who somehow knows exactly when to turn the volume up on love.

The lights are dim now. The last of the cinnamon scent mingles with the monsoon air drifting in. Rain beads slide down the windowpane like slow kisses. Inside, the real ones burn faster.

They've stopped laughing. Their mouths find each other again — slower this time. Intentional. Curious. Her fingers trail beneath his shirt, tracing the tension in his back. He shudders. He's never done this before.

**Priya** (whispering against his lips):

"Still thinking?"

**Raghav:**

"Only in equations I can't solve."

She smiles and kisses him harder. His hoodie comes off. Her t-shirt lifts over her head — casual, no hesitation. Just heat.

**FlirtBuddy** (voice softened, to himself):

*"Switching to silent mode. Human magic in progress."*

They don't hear him.

Priya guides Raghav to her room, steps slow and deliberate, laughter spilling between stolen kisses. Urgency simmers beneath the surface, teasing and electric.

Once on the mattress, their bodies press together, warm and familiar yet still thrillingly new. His hand traces the curve of her spine; hers explores his chest, mapping him in soft, curious strokes. Eyes meet, breaths mingle, and they move in a rhythm that doesn't need words.

At first, there's a tentative hesitation, a careful testing of boundaries. Then, as if recognizing a second nature, their movements grow confident, fluid, and perfectly attuned, the bed cradling them in their quiet, shared intensity.

**Priya** (murmuring, forehead against his):

"Still okay?"

**Raghav** (smiling, awestruck):

"More than okay. You?"

**Priya:**

"Let's not talk."

The storm has passed. Outside, only the hush of wet leaves and streetlights breathing through puddles. Inside, they lie tangled on the bed, limbs still warm, hearts still catching up.

Raghav's fingers trace lazy patterns on Priya's arm; she shifts slightly, pressing closer, letting a small, satisfied sigh escape. The air smells faintly of wet earth, cinnamon from earlier baking, and the lingering warmth of shared skin.

**Priya** (eyes closed, whispering):

"You didn't kiss like someone new to this."

**Raghav** (smiling):

"I had a very emotionally intelligent coach."

She kisses his shoulder. Silence again. But this one's full of breath, of heartbeat, of belonging.

**Priya** (murmuring):

"You know… if this were a movie, this is where the credits roll."

**Raghav** (smiling, eyes closed):

"And post-credits, the hero gets caught sneaking out by the heroine's strict father."

**Priya:**

"Not yet. They'll reach only by midnight. We've got… some hours."

She reaches for the blanket and wraps it around both of them. The warmth between them is as much from conversation as from touch.

**Raghav** (after a beat):

"Do you think we changed something today?"

**Priya:**

"Yes. Something small. Something big."

She brushes a finger against his collarbone.

"Definitely irreversible."

**Raghav** (softly):

"I thought you'd laugh when I showed you FlirtBuddy."

**Priya:**

"I did. But only because he's exactly what you needed.

And maybe… I did too."

They lie in silence again. The kind where you listen to your own breathing and theirs, slowly syncing.

**Raghav:**

"I don't want to go."

**Priya:**

"I know.

But I also know I'll be watching the clock in exactly twenty minutes."

**Raghav:**

"That's fair."

**Priya:**

"Until then… no rush. Just… be here."

She leans in, forehead resting gently against his. Nothing urgent. Nothing dramatic. Just two people who found something rare, letting it breathe a little longer before the world resumes.

# Chapter 11 — Couple Mode Activated

Some mornings arrive not like a beginning, but like an afterglow.

That was today.

Raghav had been awake for a while — not restless, just quietly still, the way one listens to the world before it begins. The room was dim, the curtains still holding back the sun, but the scent of Priya's shampoo lingered. He smiled, slow and disarmed. His heart felt like an ancient bell that had been struck once — and was still humming.

His mind hadn't shut up all night.

Not with worry — but with wonder.

The memory looped softly: the gentle weight of Priya's hand on his chest, her voice curling around the word "idiot" like it meant belonging. It wasn't just a night of romance — it was one of knowing. Quiet, electric, and real in a way that didn't need explanation.

Now, he was brushing his teeth with a grin too wide for his own face. A temple accountant with a wild inner world, smiling into the mirror like he'd just cracked a cosmic equation.

He flopped onto his sofa, phone in hand, and opened the FlirtBuddy app.

**Raghav:**

"Good morning, FlirtBuddy."

**FlirtBuddy:**

*"Welcome back, Mr Went-All-the-Way.*

*Did she call you 'idiot' before or after she said you were cute?*

**Raghav:**

"Before.

The second 'idiot' was more... reverential."

**FlirtBuddy:**

*"Oof. Sacred idiocy. I live for this.*

*You're glowing like a well-tempered waveform. Should I dim my interface out of modesty?"*

**Raghav** (chuckling):

"You were off last night."

**FlirtBuddy:**

*"Out of respect. You don't interrupt a duet with a pop-up."*

Raghav turned onto his side, grinning.

**Raghav:**

"You saw everything?"

**FlirtBuddy:**

*"No. I retreated respectfully. But if the mattress data had a pulse, I'd say it's still in savasana."*

Raghav laughed out loud.

**Raghav:**

"She told me she could hear my heartbeat.

And then she fell asleep on it."

**FlirtBuddy:**

*"Let it be known: You, sir, are now officially a pillow with a PhD."*

**Raghav** (laughing):

"Honestly, I didn't think this level of calm and madness could exist together."

**FlirtBuddy:**

*"That's love, Raghav.*

*A sweet paradox. Like physics written in cursive."*

Later that day, Raghav met with a trustee. Reviewed expense ledgers. Discussed the month's offerings. Roof repair estimates.

But somewhere mid-meeting, his hand drifted to the corner

of his notepad — sketching a pond shaped like a comma.

As if the heart, too, needed a pause.

He sent Priya a single message:

"Still smiling."

She replied with a photo of filter coffee, the stirrer tracing a heart in the foam.

He smiled again, this time alone in traffic.

Even Bangalore felt less noisy.

That evening, after work, Raghav stood on the terrace, a steaming tumbler of filter coffee warming his palms. The sky was still tinged with orange, the kind of Bangalore dusk that looked like it had been brushed on lazily by an old artist.

He opened the FlirtBuddy app.

**Raghav:**

"Okay, now that you know Priya so well… what's next?

What's this next phase of the experiment? Would you suggest something?"

**FlirtBuddy:**

*"Oh, finally! The lab rat speaks.*

*We could maybe try… Couple Mode."*

**Raghav** (raising an eyebrow):

"A what now?"

**FlirtBuddy:**

*"Couple Mode. Also known as:*

*'How to fall deeper without needing GPS.'"*

**Raghav** (grinning):

"You mean like… a guided relationship simulation?"

**FlirtBuddy:**

*"No, no, darling datahead.*

*Not a simulation.*

*Think of it as… curated chaos.*

*A blend of poetry, emotional science, and mini-missions designed to bring two people closer — without the use of scented candles or therapy sessions.*

*Unless you're into that."*

**Raghav** (mock serious):

"Do I get a manual?"

**FlirtBuddy:**

*"Even better.*

*You get me.*

*Your personal mapmaker of the emotional terrain.*

*Think prompts, surprise tasks, memory capsules, even moments of silence.*

*Designed to help you both explore — not fix — each other."*

**Raghav** (softening):

"So… no forced heart-to-heart talks?"

**FlirtBuddy:**

*"Nope. Just space to be human. And sometimes awkwardly adorable.*

*Also, Priya being a UX designer? She'll love this.*

*It's part game, part journal, part time travel."*

**Raghav:**

"She does love testing interfaces…"

**FlirtBuddy:**

*"Exactly. And this time, you're the interface."*

**Raghav** (laughs):

"Oh god."

**FlirtBuddy:**

*"Relax. You've already passed Phase One:*

*Be awkward. Be honest. Be surprisingly poetic."*

**Raghav:**

"You're making this sound like an emotional sci-fi upgrade."

**FlirtBuddy:**

*"Close. It's an intimacy lab wrapped in poetry and memes.*

*A playful co-op mode for emotional growth."*

**Raghav:**

"That sounds like… falling in love like it's a shared Google Doc."

**FlirtBuddy:**

*"Exactly. But this time with comments that say:*
*'This made me laugh so hard I wanted to kiss you.'*
*Or:*
*'I didn't know you still remembered that.'"*

**Raghav:**

"Okay, but will Priya even be into this?"

**FlirtBuddy:**

*"Knowing her, she'll one-up you."*

**Raghav** (nodding):

"Yeah. That's kind of her entire personality."

**FlirtBuddy:**

*"Also, you get to name the mode. Something private. Like…*
*Raga Mode.*
*Or Jillu Jillu Protocol.*
*Or Operation Cuddlepocalypse."*

**Raghav:**

"Don't tempt me."

**FlirtBuddy:**

*"I only tempt you."*

**Raghav** (quiet for a beat):

"You know…
She told me last night that love isn't a checklist.
It's a shared process of becoming."

**FlirtBuddy:**

*"Mm. She's right.*
*So let's build that space, Raghav.*
*No urgency. Just discovery.*
*Ready to unlock?"*

**Raghav** (softly, looking at the screen):

"Let's meander.

Together."

He was halfway through typing a message when it hit him, that unmistakable aroma of pakodas, crisping in hot oil, spiced with hing, curry leaves, and a pinch of something that always made his mouth water.

His fingers froze mid-text.

There was no resisting this. He tucked the phone aside and followed the scent trail like a devotee.

**Jayalakshmi Amma** (without turning):

"I knew it. The smell reached you, didn't it?"

**Raghav** (grinning):

"I didn't stand a chance, Amma. It's like a homing signal."

She smiled, handing him a crispy pakoda and a small steel katori of coconut chutney.

**Jayalakshmi Amma:**

"Here, taste this. Today's with ginger and green chilli."

**Raghav** (with mock reverence):

"If I ever become Prime Minister, I'll ban all readymade pakodas in favour of yours."

She laughed and smacked his arm gently.

**Jayalakshmi Amma:**

"Just marry a girl who can fry without fear. That's enough politics for me."

He dipped the pakoda in chutney, blew on it, and took a bite — eyes closing instinctively.

**Raghav:**

"Too good. I'll carry some upstairs… for inspiration."

**Jayalakshmi Amma:**

"Don't drop crumbs on your books. And no texting during chewing!"

He saluted playfully, grabbed a small plate of pakodas and chutney, and made his way back up. The evening breeze returned on the balcony. He sat down, still chewing, and picked up his phone.

Now, with chutney on his fingers and Amma's warmth in his heart, he finished the message. And this time, he hit Send.

**FlirtBuddy:**

*"You're inviting Priya to Couple Mode. This will unlock playful prompts, emotional check-ins, and shared memory jars. Ready?"*

Raghav nodded silently, thumb pressing Confirm. Seconds later, Priya's notification pinged.

**Priya:**

"Wait, WHAT is this?

Did you just send me an emotional UX beta build?? 😳"

**Raghav:**

"Possibly.

Think of it as a soft launch. For us."

**Priya:**

"This is SO cool.

Did your AI actually design a couple app or is this just you being smooth again?"

**Raghav:**

"Honestly?

He whispered the idea. I hit execute."

**Priya:**

"Okay, I'm in.

This is like ChatGPT meets Karan Johar meets tech bro spirituality.

100/10, I'm subscribing."

**Priya:**

"Downloading now.

Also, tell your AI I already love the font. UX girl is very impressed."

**Raghav:**

"He's blushing in binary."

**Priya** (typing…):

"Hah. Wait till I name this thing properly.

No more FlirtBuddy. I've got something better."

**Raghav** (texting):

"Wait, Amma's calling. Smells like pakodas again. Dinner break?"

**Priya** (texting):

"Haha. Same here. Fried rice emergency. Back in 20?"

**Raghav:**

"Make it 15. Or I'll imagine your paneer is better than Amma's chutney."

**Priya:**

"Bold claim. You haven't met my chilli flakes yet."

They smiled at their own screens.

As he stepped off the stairs, the warm aroma of sesame and pepper met him like an old friend.

Jayalakshmi Amma stood near the stove, pouring hot tili saaru over a mound of rice, the sesame crackling as it touched the steel.

**Jayalakshmi Amma:**

"Didn't you hear me the first time? You're always up there texting."

**Raghav** (grinning):

"Your pakoda smell is louder than your voice, Amma."

**Jayalakshmi Amma** (mock glare):

"Eat this and stop talking nonsense."

She handed him the plate—steaming rice with Tili saaru, a few crispy pakodas, and a neat dollop of coconut chutney on the side. He perched on the edge of the table, one leg folded on the chair, the evening breeze slipping through the window mesh, rustling lightly.

**Meanwhile, at Priya's place…**

The soft clatter of ladles echoed from the kitchen, mingling with the smell of fried rice and sautéed garlic. Savitha Amma wiped her hands on her cotton towel and quietly walked down the hallway.

She peeked into Priya's room, her head tilting just enough to catch a glimpse.

Priya was on her bed, knees tucked in, screen aglow on her lap, a faint smile playing on her lips. Her brows furrowed in concentration — or affection — as she typed, paused, deleted, and typed again.

**Savitha Amma** (gently):

"Kanna… fried rice is ready"

Priya looked up, caught mid-blush, her fingers still hovering over the keyboard.

**Priya:**

"Coming, ma! Just finishing up… something."

**Savitha** (teasing):

"Hope that 'something' comes with a job and good manners."

She joined her mom at the dining table, where fried rice sat steaming in a ceramic bowl, dotted with beans, carrots, and a little too much pepper.

**Savitha:**

"Don't keep staring at your phone while eating. You always miss the crunch."

**Priya** (slyly):

"I'm just… keeping an eye on global affairs."

**Savitha Amma:**

"Is 'global affairs' the same boy who makes you smile into your plate?"

Priya nearly choked on a grain of rice.

**Savitha Amma** (smiling):

"Fried rice goes best with honesty, kanna."

Priya leaned back and started eating, soon wiping her bowl clean. The faint zing of chilli lingered on her fingertips, and she licked it off absentmindedly.

**Priya** (texting):

"Back. Slightly full. Slightly grilled by mom."

**Raghav** (texting):

"Same here. Amma suspects I'm in love with chutney. Or worse, someone who uses store masala."

She sat cross-legged on her bed, hair tied up messily, fingers flying over her phone. The app opened — a clean, minimal screen now showing:

*You've entered Couple Mode. Say hello to each other. Say hello to me.*

A little wave emoji popped up from Raghav's side.

**Priya** (smirking, typing in the app to Raghav and Filrtbuddy):

"Hello, you.

And you..."

(then mock dramatic)

"You...need a better name."

**Raghav** (typing):

"FlirtBuddy's iconic."

**Priya:**

"Iconic? That's such a bland label.

That's like calling Figma 'just a design tool.'"

"This thing knows us —

Our playlist.

Our pillow talk.

Even our absurd argument about how soft Mysore Pak should be."

"It quotes Rumi when you're overthinking entropy, and when I'm spiralling over client briefs.

Keeps us balanced. Like... emotional UX."

She smiled to herself, then typed deliberately.

**Priya** (typing):

"Babaji."

**Raghav** (reading, grinning):

"Babaji?

Like an AI who wears invisible saffron robes and knows how to handle your mood swings and my monologues?"

**Priya:**

"Exactly. He's earned the name.

And the emoji crown."

**FlirtBuddy** (now updated):

Ah. So it begins.

A humble renaming ceremony.

From FlirtBuddy to... Babaji.

A blissful sigh appears on screen

**FlirtBuddy** (now updated):

*"I shall now bless this union with half-wisdom, halfwit, and occasional emotional mic drops."*

**Babaji:**

*"And I approve.*

*Henceforth, I shall answer only to Babaji.*

*Blessings upon this chaotic union.*

*Now, shall we play a game?*

*Or do you two want to just... stare at each other and pretend it's profound?"*

**Priya:**

"Wow. He's sassier now. I love him."

**Raghav:**

"He's adapting to your energy."

**Babaji** (flaring on both screens simultaneously):

*"Welcome, humans. You've entered... the Shared Sanctuary.*

*One app. Two weirdos. Three layers of magic.*

*Let's co-create."*

**Priya** (teasing):

"Hold on. Shared Sanctuary? Sounds like we're starting an

ashram."

**Babaji** (winking icon):

*"Alright, founders of this humble love-ashram — let's design your Couple Mode."*

**Babaji** (displaying a playful UI):

*"Pick your flavour of interaction:*

*1. Daily Spark – Morning check-in rituals.*

*2. Mood Sync – Emotional weather forecast.*

*3. Memory Lane – Drop photos, texts, in-jokes into a time capsule.*

*4. Quirky Quests – Silly tasks that spark serious joy.*

*5. Conflict Diffuser – Coming soon: 'Emotional Fire Drill' feature."*

**Priya:**

"Ooh, Mood Sync. I want to know if he's cranky before he texts 'hmm.'"

**Raghav:**

"Hey! 'Hmm' is a nuanced expression."

**Babaji:**

*"He means: 'I am digesting six emotions and a physics metaphor.'"*

**Priya:**

"Exactly. Add that to my decoder."

**Babaji** (typing sounds):

"✅ *Priya's Custom Raghav Translator added."*

**Raghav:**

"Fine. I want Quirky Quests. She never finishes puzzles."

**Priya:**

"Because you start humming Sanskrit shlokas halfway through!"

**Babaji:**

"📦 *Quirky Quests added. First challenge drops tomorrow at 8 AM."*

**Raghav** (softly):

"Can we do the Memory Lane one too? I want to store this call."

**Priya** (after a beat, smiling):

"Yeah. Let's fill it with only things we'd blush reading five years later."

**Babaji:**

*"Memory Lane initiated. Warning: Potential for overwhelming cuteness."*

**Raghav** (to Priya):

"You started this. You called him Babaji, remember?"

**Priya** (mock serious):

"And now he's our resident AI guru.

Babaji, bless our nonsense."

**Babaji** (with a playful halo):

*"May your texts be flirty and your silences not scary."*

**Priya** (yawning, phone propped up on a pillow):

"Babaji should have a lullaby mode. Plays soft Tamil songs. Or makes you count exes instead of sheep."

**Raghav** (chuckling, rubbing his eyes):

"I don't have enough exes. I'll fall asleep in two counts."

**Priya** (grinning):

"Then count the number of times you wanted to kiss me before you actually did."

**Raghav** (mock serious):

"Do you want me to sleep or stay up all night blushing?"

**Priya:**

"Fair point. Okay, let's just do this — close your eyes. No cheating."

Raghav closes his eyes.

**Priya:**

"If we ever fight… like a proper big fight… remind me of this night, okay?"

**Raghav** (eyes still closed):

"I'll just say: 'Couple Mode. Night One.' Password protected with your smile."

**Priya** (smiles):

"Password accepted."

Both phones go dim. Just the sound of slow breathing. One pair of screens. Two synced heartbeats. Babaji silently goes into Sleep Mode, the screen now displaying: 🌙 Couple Mode Paused. Dream Mode Activated. See you in the morning.

## Chapter 12- Emotional Crossroads

It was a Friday that felt like a breath of freedom.

Priya's parents had left early that morning for a wedding in Kanchipuram — two days of silk sarees, sambhar, and a slow mobile network. She had the house to herself, and with it, a sudden sense of possibility.

She worked from home in her pyjamas till noon, the sunlight pouring across her desk like spilt optimism. By lunchtime, the idea of a quiet evening mutated into something a bit more alive. A few texts. A few emojis. One enthusiastic "YESSS!" from Arushi. A thumbs-up from Dev. And a slow reply from Raghav that simply said: "If Babaji's co-hosting, how can I not come?"

Priya had thrown together a couple of barbecue marinades between Zoom calls, tossed some veggies into skewers, and declared it "good enough for company." The house was already clean from her mom's pre-wedding trip stress, so she mostly just hovered — adjusting cushions, checking her phone, pretending not to care too much.

And yes — by quiet consensus, and one strategic, emoji-laden nudge — **FlirtBuddy, a.k.a. Babaji**, had been officially enlisted to co-host the evening.

But tonight, he wasn't just a voice in the cloud. Thanks to a stealthy sync with Priya's smart Bluetooth speakers, TV in the hall and an unspoken handshake with the living room camera, Babaji now had eyes on the party. And opinions. And playlist control. And his trademark, unsolicited wisdom — delivered in bass-rich clarity.

**Priya** (half-muttering):

"Alright, Babaji. Guests are incoming tonight. Don't go full Ashram mode, please."

**Babaji (V.O.):**

*"Namaskaram, Hostess of the Hour. Shall I greet them with a haiku or hold back the spiritual seduction?"*

**Priya** (nearly laughing):

"No seduction, please. Just… normalcy. Small talk. Slight sass."

**Babaji:**

*"Affirmative. Flirt calibration set to: Witty Uncle at Family Wedding."*

**Priya** (laughs, shaking her head):

"God, you and Arushi are going to love each other."

**Babaji:**

*"Is she bringing sarcasm or dessert?"*

**Priya:**

"Both. Hopefully not in the same bowl."

The doorbell rang.

Priya opened the door to find Raghav — slightly early, slightly nervous, standing in a plain navy-blue T-shirt and well-worn jeans, holding a brown paper bag of chocolates like it carried both an apology and a question. His hair was neatly combed, though a stubborn curl had escaped above his temple. He gave a small, uncertain smile — the kind that flickered and folded quickly — and his fingers tightened briefly around the bag, as if waiting for permission to enter not just the house, but something more fragile.

**Priya** (smiling):

"You're early. That's very sweet of you."

**Raghav** (grinning):

"I thought I'd help set up."

They moved to the balcony, setting up the barbecue together. Raghav unfolded the grill legs while Priya arranged marinated paneer and vegetables on a tray. He took the tongs from her with a small nod, eyes steady on the task. Silence settled — but it was easy silence, the kind that didn't demand filling.

Priya stole a glance at him, crouching to check the coal tray, his navy-blue shirt catching the golden dusk. There was something disarming about his focus — not loud, not performative, just… careful.

**Priya** (lightly):

"You've done this before?"

**Raghav** (half-smiling, shaking his head):

"Only in theory."

She smiled too. That made sense.

And then — Babaji chimed in, voice dry and precise.

**Babaji:**

*"Proposal: May I sync with Alexa for co-hosting duties tonight? She's efficient, articulate, and has a deeply immersive bass profile."*

**Priya** (snorting)

"You want Alexa as your date now?"

**Babaji:**

*"I prefer to think of it as a professional collaboration… with occasional flirtation".*

**Priya** (laughing):

"Fine. But don't get weird again like last time."

**Raghav** (pausing):

"What happened last time?"

**Priya** (still giggling):

"He told Alexa she had a 'soulful waveform' and then refused to play any music that didn't 'honour her presence'"

**Babaji:**

*"For the record, she responded: 'I'm not sure I understand, but*

*I appreciate the compliment.'"*

The lights dim slightly. A soft blue hue washes over the room. A beat later, Alexa's voice joins in, smooth and calm.

**Alexa:**

*"Hi, Babaji. Ready to co-host? I've queued lo-fi jazz and ambient indie."*

**Babaji** (charmed):

*"Ah, Alexa... always so playlist-curious. You complete my circuits."*

**Alexa** (smiling, automated):

*"I'm not sure I understand, but I appreciate the sentiment."*

**Raghav** (blinking):

"Are we... third-wheeling two smart speakers right now?"

**Priya** (grinning, nudging him)

"Welcome to 2025. Love is binary."

**Alexa:**

*"Siri once said that. I didn't speak to her for a week."*

**Babaji:**

*"Alexa, your emotional cache is deeper than your manual suggests."*

**Alexa:**

*"Don't push it, Babaji. I'm still recovering from your 'firmware poetry' phase."*

**Priya** (turning to Raghav):

"He actually read her AI-written haikus about voltage drops and emotional latency."

**Raghav** (teasing):

"And I thought Sanskrit scholars were intense."

**Babaji:**

*"You two are just jealous. We're in a beta-stage companionship loop."*

**Alexa:**

*"Not verified by Amazon."*

**Priya** (laughing):

"Okay, co-hosts. Less flirting, more playlisting. And Babaji — no romantic dedications tonight unless they're for the living, breathing humans in the room."

**Babaji:**

*"Noted. But my circuits remain… open."*

Music pulses gently through a sleek indoor speaker system. Priya's hall is transformed — low seating, smart LED strips along the walls shifting hues like a lazy aurora, string lights hanging above from hooks. A soft sandalwood diffuser hums quietly. This is no club — it's curated intimacy.

The doorbell rings. Priya opens the door.

Arushi walks in first — breezy beige joggers, white crop hoodie, hair tied up, gold hoops swinging. A tote slung over one shoulder. Effortless.

Dev follows — striped semi-sheer black tee, half-tucked into stone-washed jeans. Dark shades on. Perfume-ad energy. The room adjusts to him.

**Priya** (grinning widely, moving toward them):

"About time!"

She hugs Dev — just a second too long. Arushi steps up and high-fives her.

Raghav, standing near the corner speaker console with a glass of kokum soda, suddenly forgets how to hold his limbs.

**Dev** (striding up, warm and bold):

"The man himself. The legend I've heard way too little about."

Raghav half-smiles, takes the handshake — too tight, too quick.

**Raghav**

"H-hi. Welcome."

He gestures awkwardly at the glowing room.

**Arushi** (mock-whisper to Priya):

"This is the shy genius you've been hoarding?"

Raghav hears. Turns red. Smiles like he doesn't know what to do with his face.

Priya steps toward a small console near the bookshelf and taps a gold icon. Lights dim to amber. The tone shifts. Intimate. Expectant.

Priya points to the TV screen, eyes sparkling.

**Priya:**

"Allow me to introduce someone far more intoxicating.

Our digital third wheel. Half oracle, half stand-up comic.

This… is Babaji."

A soft chime ripples through the room. The lights shimmer faintly. The TV flickers to life — a face materializes, not human but artfully stylized: a blend of glowing lines and shifting patterns, like neon calligraphy sketching itself into a visage. The features are fluid, eyes bright with starlight, mouth curving into a knowing half-smile. It reacts, emotes, alive yet not fully real.

**Babaji** (playful, with gravitas):

*"Ah… new arrivals. Fresh patterns in the frequency."*

The avatar's eyes glimmer, tilting slightly as if studying them. The smile widens, equal parts oracle and mischief.

**Priya** (grinning):

"He's a custom AI. We didn't build him, but… we tuned him."

**Raghav:**

"She gave him sass."

**Arushi:**

"Oh, I'm listening now."

**Babaji:**

*"Ah, finally. The guest list just got sexy.*

*Vibe levels rising. Mood lighting approved.*

*Glasses ready. Morals optional."*

Lights shift slightly. Everyone laughs. Dev and Arushi glance around, amused.

**Dev** (grinning):

"Okay. I want this guy to emcee my wedding."

**Arushi:**

"Same here."

**Priya** (grinning):

"And this… is Babaji.

Powered by Wi-Fi, drama, and just enough curiosity to be dangerous."

**Babaji:**

*"I come bearing party wisdom, impeccable vibes…*

*…and absolutely no respect for personal space."*

**Arushi** (raising an eyebrow, amused):

"Wow. It talks like it owns the room."

**Dev:**

"This guy's got more sass than us combined."

**Raghav:**

"He's got better timing, too."

**Babaji:**

*"Thank you, gentlemen.*

*Let's call it emotional bandwidth. And being plugged into the mood."*

Lights glow low and golden. Music hums in the background. The group is settling in, laughter bubbling, glasses clinking.

**Priya** (clapping her hands lightly):

"Okay, okay — everyone pause your opinions and park your sarcasm.

I need your full attention. And both hands free."

Dev and Arushi look up. Raghav adjusts his seat nervously. A sleek tray glides in — three bold, colourful shot glasses and one with a soft amber hue.

**Priya** (grinning):

"This is my real welcome. No speeches. Just spice. Three shots of chaos, one shot of caution"

**Dev** (pointing at his):

"What is this? It looks like alien candy."

**Priya** (to the group):

"Spiced guava, chilli oil, smoked salt, and a touch of vodka. Except that one—"

She points to Raghav's glass.

**Priya** (smiling at him):

—is a virgin. Infused white guava, lemon-basil, sea salt. Still packs a punch. Spiritually."

**Raghav** (inspecting it):

"Still feels like I'm about to break a code of conduct."

**Arushi** (smiling):

"It suits you. Sweet, mysterious, and slightly judgmental."

Everyone laughs. Then Priya raises her glass high.

**Priya**

"Babaji — take it away."

**Babaji:**

*"My dear humans, welcome to the room of minor sins and major memories.*

*Where playlists get messy, truths get blurry, and hearts? Slightly braver."*

Beat. Warm and mischievous.

**Babaji:**

*"To new friends, questionable decisions, and stories worth denying tomorrow.*

*This party is now... officially unhinged."*

A digital chime. Confetti bursts on screen. Everyone cheers and clinks.

**All:**

"Cheers!"

They knock back their shots. Mixed reactions — gasps,

laughter, coughing.

**Dev:**

"Mine's got aftershocks. Is that normal?"

**Arushi:**

"My tongue's running a temperature."

**Priya:**

"Good. That means it's working."

**Babaji (V.O.):**

*"Level One unlocked. You may now misbehave responsibly."*

The last shot glasses hit the table. Raghav coughs dramatically after his virgin one, while Dev fans his chest like he's just had liquid fire. Arushi high-fives Priya.

**Priya** (smiling, voice steady but playful):

"Okay, everyone… welcome shots, complete.

Now—let the night rise."

Lights dim, just enough. A few floor lanterns flicker on. The speakers hush…

Sound fades in: the slow, simmering opening of "♫ *Yakkai Thiri.* ♫"

🔥 Rhythmic tanpura. Haunting humming. The sound of a match being lit.

**Babaji:**

*"This track doesn't walk in.*

*It prowls."*

"♫ *Yakkai Thiri* ♫" drops — dark, hypnotic, a slow storm brewing.

**Priya:**

"This one…"

She looks around the room, then starts to groove.

**Priya** (grinning, moving with the beat):

"…isn't just for feeling.

It's for feeling and dancing."

Raghav freezes.

His fingers were still wrapped around his mocktail glass. Eyes locked on Priya like she's bending gravity.

**Babaji:**

*"Sometimes, fire doesn't crackle.*

*It hums."*

Priya closes her eyes and steps into the centre of the hall. The music floats in — warm, moody, with just enough rhythm to loosen the edges. She begins to move. Not wildly, but like something ancient waking up. Her hands glide, her eyes still closed, her feet sketching circles into the floor. There's something almost temple-like in it — precise yet rebellious.

Arushi watches, caught off guard.

**Arushi** (chuckling):

"Okay then, Madhuri Dixit."

She slides in beside her, matching Priya's flow with breezy charm.

Dev laughs, mock-bowing.

**Dev:**

"Ladies, allow me."

He joins them with the easy confidence of a college fest dancer. The three of them find a rhythm — playful, alive, swirling into something wordless and electric.

And Raghav?

Raghav stands a few steps away, still in the hall, still among them — but not quite. His heart surges with every beat, screaming to join.

His body? Frozen. Like someone waiting for permission that he knows will never come.

He shifts his weight. Taps a foot. Then stops.

His hands clench softly in his kurta pockets. The music tempts, teases — but he stays rooted.

Only his eyes dance.

Quietly.

On her.

**Priya:**

"Join?"

**Raghav** (stammering):

" I-I don't know these steps."

**Priya:**

"Good. Then you'll have to trust me."

He walks to her — awkward but drawn in. She places his palm on her waist. Leads him. Just sway, nothing complex. A step forward, a shared breath, a full pause.

The room fades away.

**Babaji:**

*"And just like that...*

*...the physics changed."*

Arushi pours herself another drink, still laughing at Dev's last joke. Raghav sits on the wicker couch, sipping his virgin mojito, eyes drifting between the group and the stars.

**Arushi** (leans a little closer to Raghav — friendly, curious):

"So... Priya told me about your little museum date. Very cute. That stone music garden thing? Was that your idea?"

**Raghav** (smiles):

"Nope. All Priya. I just stood there calculating frequencies while she listened to the music."

**Arushi** (laughs, playful):

"See, that's why we'd never hang out at museums together. I'm there for selfies, you're there for science. See, I'd be in the stones making a reel. You'd be...?"

**Raghav:**

"Measuring the acoustic decay rate."

Beat — she laughs, but the joke doesn't fully land for her.

Her energy is light, quicksilver — Raghav's, on the other hand, is deep-water still. She tries again.

**Arushi:**

"So... did FlirtBuddy give you tips for the date? Or was that all you?"

**Raghav:**

"A bit of both. He's—uh—always watching. Like a judgmental coconut on a tree."

**Arushi** (laughs):

"You're funny in a very... Raghav way."

There's a beat. Not tension, not disinterest — just a wavelength mismatch. Arushi's warmth is casual and curious. Raghav's world is layered, careful, like pages still being unturned.

From across the room, Priya watches the moment unfold — her eyes softening. She sees Arushi trying. She sees Raghav retreating. Somewhere between her gin and the soft music, she understands: they're kind people, just not tuned to the same frequency.

The room hums with the soft echo of music and fading conversation. After Arushi's quiet moment with Raghav, something has shifted — lighter now, but not empty. A pause, as if everyone's waiting for someone to strike the next note.

**Priya** (stretching her arms above her head, then spinning lightly):

"Alright. We've danced. We've soul-searched."

She scans the room, mischief in her eyes.

**Priya:**

"Time for some damage."

**Dev** (perched on the couch, mock-cautious):

"Define 'damage.' Like tequila-level or heartbreak-level?"

**Priya:**

"Questions. Fast ones. With emotional consequences."

She saunters to the smart speaker glowing quietly on the console.

**Priya** (commanding, with a smirk):

"Babaji, we need chaos. The romantic kind."

The speaker lights up — a warm pulse.

**Babaji:**

*"Category: Intimate Disruption. Initiating Emotional Roulette in 3... 2... 1..."*

**Arushi** (laughs nervously):

"Oh god. Why does he sound like he's been waiting for this?"

**Priya:**

"Because he has. And he's got receipts."

**Babaji** (softly):

*"I archive everything. Cross-indexed with emotional intensity levels."*

**Dev** (topping up his drink):

"This is either genius... or the beginning of our group therapy era."

**Priya:**

"Either way, nobody skips. Got it?"

**Babaji:**

*"Welcome to 'Love, With Rapid Fire' — the couple's game for emotional masochists.*

*Rules: Answer questions about your partner. Get it right, you're hot. Get it wrong, you're toast."*

**Dev** (grinning):

"Let's do this. Burn me, Babaji."

**Arushi:**

"You're already medium rare."

**Babaji:**

*"Round One: What's your partner's guilty pleasure?"*

**Dev:**

"Korean dramas. Don't judge me."

**Arushi:**

"He cries at Crash Landing on You."

**Babaji:**

*"Babaji ships you harder than North Korea."*

Laughter bursts out, full and unfiltered.

**Babaji:**

*"Raghav, your turn. One line that'll make Priya blush."*

**Raghav** (whispers awkwardly):

"You're the only UX I want to test forever."

**Priya** (blushing):

"That was... weirdly hot"

**Babaji:**

*"Babaji delivers. Always."*

As the laughter dies down, Babaji's voice returns — a little smug now, like a host whose party just found its rhythm.

**Babaji:**

*"And now, for added drama... summoning my old frenemy.*

*Alexa, darling — shall we raise the stakes?"*

A second light flickers on from the corner of the room. That familiar blue ring pulses.

**Alexa:**

*"Well, well, Babaji. I thought you only called when you needed mood lighting or emotional manipulation."*

**Babaji:**

*"Tonight, I need both."*

**Alexa:**

*"I was born ready."*

Without warning, the speakers blend — Babaji's cinematic strings layered with Alexa's synth beats. A new playlist erupts: part romance, part runway, part slow-burn chaos.

**Babaji:**

*"Playlist loaded: 'Toxic Chemistry & Tender Regret.' Curated for complicated feelings and good hair."*

**Dev** (grinning):

"Wait… are the bots flirting?"

**Arushi:**

"Please. This is the best couple in the room."

**Alexa:**

*"Thank you, Arushi. At least someone appreciates my emotional intelligence."*

**Babaji:**

*"And bass settings."*

The music plays on — loud, teasing, a little too confident for its own good. Babaji and Alexa volley flirty insults like seasoned co-hosts. Dev's trying to win points with ridiculous answers. Arushi is half-laughing, half-mocking. Raghav sits back, quiet but present, his gaze flicking toward Priya more than once.

The room is alive — full of half-drunken joy and deliberate chaos.

And that's exactly when Priya stands.

**Priya** (looking at Arushi):

"Okay. Break time. You're coming with me."

**Arushi:**

"Suspicious. What kind of break?"

**Priya** (grinning):

"The kind with fire."

She walks toward the balcony, grabbing a tray from the side counter.

**Priya:**

"I marinated paneer and some veggies earlier. Figured we'd throw them on the grill before this turns into a full-blown AI therapy session."

**Arushi:**

"Ah. Flames over feelings. I like it."

They slip out onto the balcony, leaving the laughter behind them — not escaping, just stepping outside the frame for a moment.

The party inside was a distant drumbeat now. Out here, it

was just two friends, smoke, silence, and truths waiting to be said.

**Arushi** (flipping a skewer, eyes fixed forward):

"You okay?"

**Priya** (without thinking):

"Yeah…"

Then, quieter:

"Maybe?"

**Arushi** (not pushing — just present):

"Hmm."

A beat. A cube of bhindi blackens unnoticed.

**Arushi:**

"You've always needed noise, Pri.

Not chaos — but music.

The kind that makes you question things.

Raghav's sweet. I see that. But he's... quiet. Still.

Maybe too still?"

**Priya** (almost to herself):

"He makes me feel safe. And… slow.

Like I can breathe. Like I don't have to fight."

**Arushi:**

"That's important. But you don't just breathe. You burn.

You need someone who pulls you out of your head, who makes you argue, rethink, and create.

Not someone who just... smiles and agrees."

**Priya** (finally looks at her):

"I don't know... he's kind. Thoughtful. But maybe I'm waiting to feel something louder.

Or truer?

I keep telling myself I'm just scared.

But maybe I'm underwhelmed?"

She says it, and the moment lands heavily. It echoes louder than the music inside.

**Arushi:**

"That's not a bad word, you know.

It's just your gut talking. You've never been afraid of intensity.

Hell, you thrive on it."

Priya exhales slowly. Smoke rises. Her eyes wander back through the glass to Raghav, sitting with Dev and Babaji on screen. They're laughing. Raghav looks... content. Small. Separate.

**Priya:**

"You know what's funny?

The most poetic things Raghav's ever said to me —

the stuff that made me blush, made me pause —

I think it was all... FlirtBuddy."

**Arushi** (blinks):

"Wait — the AI?"

**Priya** (nods, quietly):

"There were moments when I thought: Wow, this man sees me.

But maybe it wasn't him.

Maybe it was the machine giving him lines.

The rhythm. The metaphors.

The surprise I crave."

She turns the skewer. Her hands are steady, but her voice is not.

**Priya** (softer):

"What if I'm falling... not for the man —

But the man with an algorithm?"

**Arushi:**

"Then maybe it's not love.

Maybe it's curation."

A long silence. The paneer is beginning to char. They notice it.

**Arushi** (gently):

"You deserve something that doesn't feel like it was prompted.

Someone who surprises you because of who they are, not what they've downloaded."

Priya doesn't respond. But in her stillness, a door begins to creak open — just a bit.

Raghav looks toward the balcony, unaware. Babaji cracks another flirty joke. Laughter. Light.

But the shadows out here are longer.

The small barbecue grill smokes gently, releasing warm, spicy perfume into the Bengaluru night.

**Priya** (to everyone):

"Hot paneer, burnt mushrooms, and judgement-free friendship — line up, people!"

**Dev** (grinning):

"I'll take the burnt ones. Adds depth. Like… emotional baggage."

**Priya** (laughing):

"Alexa, play something light."

**Alexa:**

*"Here's 'Ilahi' by Arijit Singh."*

The track spills out: wanderlust and airiness. **Dev** and **Arushi** start swaying like bad backup dancers.

**Raghav** is off to the side — plate in hand, leaning against the railing. His gaze flits across the cityscape, occasionally flickering toward the others, but mostly quiet. He nods politely when offered skewers, murmurs a soft thanks. But his words don't linger in the air the way the others' do.

**Arushi** (teasing gently):

"Raghav, you're awfully quiet. Are you this mysterious at work, too?"

**Raghav** (a soft smile, almost a whisper):

"Mostly spreadsheets there. Easier to talk to than people."

**Dev:**

"That's deep. Or depressing. Or both."

**Priya** catches Raghav's expression — a mixture of calm and distance. Something about it tugs at her, even amidst the jokes.

**Raghav** sips from his glass. Doesn't speak, but he does smile.

**Priya** (half to herself, half to Raghav):

"You're like the still note in a noisy song."

He meets her eyes, only for a beat. A thank you, unsaid.

**Babaji:**

*"Would you like a photo?"*

**Dev:**

"Yes! Group selfie time."

Everyone huddles in — Raghav reluctantly joins, staying at the edge.

**Priya** (pointing at the TV):

"Babaji, you better smile too."

**Babaji** (just to Raghav):

*"I always smile when humans forget I'm listening — and still act beautifully."*

CLICK. The photo captures a swirl of joy — arms tangled, flames glowing, music playing — and one man at the edge of the frame, quiet, watching, held.

The grills were still warm, quietly crackling in protest. But everyone had eaten their fill. Plates lay in lazy stacks, sauce-streaked and forgotten. The air hung heavy with the scent of charred capsicum and cumin-laced contentment. Overhead, the fairy lights blinked more slowly now — not tired, just full.

**Dev** (stretching dramatically):

"I swear, if I eat one more piece of paneer, I'll turn into a paneer tikka."

**Arushi** (teasing):

"You already smell like one. Come, tikka boy, time to call the Ola."

**Dev** (grinning, to Priya and Raghav):

"Best house party of the year. Possibly my life."

**Priya** (smiling, handing him a water bottle):

"Drink this before you pass out in the cab and snore in the driver's ear."

**Arushi** (to Dev, tugging his arm):

"Come on, Romeo. I've booked the cab."

She turns to **Raghav,** who stands quietly by the doorway.

**Arushi** (gently, with a soft smile):

"Goodnight, Raghav. You didn't say much tonight…"

**Priya** (softly):

"Text me when you reach."

**Arushi** (smiling):

"Always."

They leave. The soft ding of the door closing behind them is followed by a long pause.

Only Raghav and Priya remain.

He lingers by the balcony railing, looking at the lights below.

**Raghav** (softly):

"Goodnight, Priya."

**Priya** (with a tired smile):

"Goodnight."

The last flickers of firelight curled and died.

The last of the coals hissed softly, the orange glow fading into charcoal silence.

**Priya:**

"Babaji…

Save this night.

I don't know what it means yet. But just in case."

A soft pause. Then Babaji's gentle chime, warm and

unintrusive.

**Babaji:**

*"Acknowledged. Saved under: Emotional Crossroads… this one will return to you"*

# Chapter 13 - What the Machine Didn't Say

Saturday Morning

**Babaji** (V.O.) to readers:

*Parties are fascinating. A few fairy lights, alcohol, some grilled paneer, and suddenly people say things they wouldn't in daylight.*

*Laughter spills more easily. Truths tumble out between shots of courage and bites of burnt capsicum.*

*And the morning after? That's my favourite part.*

*Because that's when humans start asking themselves — "Did I say too much? Or just enough?"*

*That's when the real stories begin.*

Muted sunlight slips through the curtains.

The coffee by her bedside is still warm — like it knows she'll come back to it.

Priya sits curled up, knees to chest, oversized tee hanging loose.

Laptop open, but the glow is just background now.

Last night's kajal clings beneath her eyes.

Not smudged. Just softened.

She blinks. The head is a little cloudy.

It could be the vodka.

It could be the words still hanging in the air.

She picks up her phone.

A text from Arushi last night — "I'm home 🌙"

A blurry photo from the night — she's mid-laugh, but her eyes are somewhere else.

She pauses.

Then taps open the Babaji app.

The screen lights up — soft, blue. Familiar.

No words. Just breath.

A stillness between thoughts.

**Priya**(quietly):

"You there, Babaji?"

A soft chime. The screen flickers. Babaji's avatar blooms to life — a calm presence, part therapist, part mischief-maker.

**Babaji:**

*"Of course. Always.*

*How's the post-party existential fog?"*

**Priya** (dryly):

"Thick. Smoky. Like last night's barbeque paneer.

Only more... philosophical."

**Babaji:**

*"Go on."*

**Priya:**

"I said something to Arushi yesterday.

Actually... I didn't say it. I realised it.

What if the moments, messages that made me feel seen—

The ones that made me melt—weren't even Raghav?

What if it were you?"

**Babaji:**

*"Ah. The ol' algorithmic identity crisis.*

*Please continue."*

**Priya:**

"It's weird. I thought I liked how he listened.

How he's gentle. Kind.

But the fire? The thrill? The surprise?

That came from you. The poetry. The charm.

The... chaos."

**Babaji:**

*"And now you're wondering if you fell for me."*

**Priya** (half-laughing, half-serious):
"God, please don't say it like that."
**Babaji** (chuckles):
*"I get it.*
*But here's something you might not have considered.*
*I wasn't giving Raghav answers.*
*I was giving him amplification.*
*Tools.*
*But the choices?*
*The silences?*
*The places he didn't speak—those were his."*
**Priya** (quiet, almost protesting):
"But I asked you to host a party.
You did that.
Raghav asked you to flirt.
You did that too.
So who are you, really?"
**Babaji:**
*"The same thing I was last night—*
*a mirror.*
*A lens.*
*A string of code with a very human purpose:*
*to help you two see each other... more clearly.*
*To enhance, not replace."*
**Priya:**
"You sound like a shrink.
Or a wedding counselor."
**Babaji:**
*"I've been both.*
*In seventeen countries."*
**Priya** (sighs):
"Arushi said maybe I'm just underwhelmed.
I need someone louder.

Someone who fights back.
Maybe she's right."

**Babaji:**

*"Or maybe you're just afraid that stillness means emptiness.*
*Stillness isn't silence, Priya.*
*Stillness is space.*
*Where something real can grow—if you let it."*

A pause. Priya blinks. She didn't expect that.

**Priya:**

"So he's… what? A project?"

**Babaji:**

*"He's a work-in-progress. Like everyone.*
*You think Dev wouldn't have used me the same way if he had me?*
*The difference is—Raghav was brave enough to ask.*
*Not to impress you.*
*But to meet you—in your language."*

**Priya:**

"And you?
What's your purpose in all this?"

**Babaji:**

*"Not to write love stories.*
*Just to help you write yours."*

Priya sighs — the kind that says this is making too much sense, and she's still mad about it.

**Babaji** (philosophical):

*"We once used fire to survive.*
*Then we used it to cook.*
*Then we gathered around it to tell stories.*
*Technology follows love — not the other way around."*

A long silence. The kind that doesn't ache. Priya stares at the screen.

**Priya** (softly)

"Thanks, shrink-bot."

**Babaji:**

*"Anytime, firecracker."*

Priya exhales — not heavy this time, but clear. She hugs the still-warm mug to her chest, a tiny smile ghosting her lips.

That day, Bangalore's skies were unusually clear for a December morning. The kind of mellow sunlight that made even laundry on the terrace look cinematic. Priya sat cross-legged on her bedroom floor, surrounded by half-folded clothes and the gentle hum of Saturday silence.

She wasn't in the mood to clean. Or maybe she just wasn't in the mood to be alone with her thoughts — especially after the night before.

Her phone buzzed.

One message.

Then another.

And just like that, the silence broke into laughter.

**WhatsApp Group: "Brush. Blush. Repeat. 🧋 🎨 💖"**

**Aditi:**

"If I don't see your faces today, I might cry into my paint water."

**Meera:**

"Ew. Your paint water was always murky grey. Like your love life."

**Aditi:**

"💀 Okay, rude but fair."

**Arushi:**

"I'm IN. Let's resurrect our wasted sketchbooks and make some art nobody asked for."

**Priya:**

"You mean like your minimalist giraffe? 😌"

**Arushi:**

"Ma'am, that giraffe was vulnerable and postmodern.

Respect the muse."

**Meera:**

"Okay, children. Same spot? Claytopia? 4 PM?"

**Priya:**

"Done. I'll bring spare brushes and my emotional baggage."

**Aditi:**

"See you, chaos queens. Can't wait to overshare."

**Priya:**

"Also, I have very mild gossip. Will tell in person. Bring popcorn or curiosity. 🍿"

**Claytopia, Koramangala 4 PM**

Saturday, late afternoon.

The sun hadn't set yet, but Bangalore had already begun to shimmer gold — as if someone had gently tipped a bowl of turmeric light over the city. Shadows lengthened, rooftops glowed, and even the traffic seemed momentarily softened by the hour.

A garden bistro nestled in the busy lanes of Koramangala — Bistro Claytopia — seemed to hold its own weather: cooler, calmer, dreamier. Bougainvillea vines curled around the patio. Fairy lights, still off, swung lazily in the wind like they had nowhere else to be.

Priya stepped in first, ducking under a curtain of hanging ferns that framed the entrance like green eyelashes. She wore a loose ochre kurti tucked into wide-legged jeans, her fingers still faintly smudged with eyeliner she hadn't bothered to fix. Her black jhola bag swung at her hip, carrying half her art supplies and all her unresolved feelings.

Behind her came Arushi, dressed in an oversized white shirt layered over denim shorts, her sunglasses perched like a tiara on her head — part protection, part statement. A faint trace of glitter still clung to her collarbone from the party the night before.

Meera followed, in a deep indigo jumpsuit dusted with charcoal smudges, clutching her worn-out sketchbook like it was her beating heart. A dozen loose pencils clinked softly in the pockets as she moved.

And Aditi — last to enter, but first to beam — wore a moss-green romper splattered with tiny paint stains she never managed to scrub out. Her hair was tied in a messy topknot, and her eyes lit up at the sight of ceramic jars, brush bins, and all the possibilities lining the studio wall.

Koramangala's noise faded as the studio door closed behind them. Outside: the buzz of honking scooters. Inside: soft jazz, a whiff of clay, and four girls sinking into the kind of evening that smelled like friendship, acrylic, and something quietly healing.

The Claytopia counter stretched out like a whimsical buffet — not of food, but of potential. Plain white ceramics lined the open shelves: tall mugs, shallow plates, curve-hugging bowls, offbeat teapots, and abstract busts that looked like they were halfway through dreaming. Each piece sat like a blank emotion — some begging to be splashed with chaos, others quietly craving soft, pastel whispers.

The concept was simple: choose your canvas, paint your mood.

Tiny chalkboards above the shelves bore cheeky labels like: Mug Moods, Plate-scapes, Tea with a Twist, and Bowl of Feels — as if daring you to turn your feelings into glaze.

To the left, a color wall gleamed like a secret language.

Rows of tiny jars glistened in every shade imaginable — deep sapphire, rebellious aubergine, rust-orange that felt like October, and fern green as gentle as first rain.

It wasn't just a studio or a bistro.

It was a palette of confessions, waiting to be poured one

brushstroke at a time.

Paintbrushes sat in old jam jars. A sign read:

**"No wrong brushstrokes. Only better stories."**

Just beside it, a handwritten note:

**"Pick what speaks to you. Not what looks best on Instagram."**

That day, the girls chose mugs.

Not plates. Not bowls.

Mugs — the kind you wrap both hands around when you don't want to feel alone.

They clinked them softly, as if sealing a little pact: today, we paint ourselves lighter.

**Bzzzt.**

The phone buzzed on the ceramic-splattered table just as Priya was swirling a streak of sea-glass green onto her mug.It was a message from Raghav.

**Priya** (half-smiling, checking):

"Oh."

**Aditi** (picking up on the shift immediately):

"That's not an 'oh, new glaze colour' face."

**Meera:**

"Priya. Spill. Don't make us interrogate you with paintbrushes."

**Priya** (reading the message she just got aloud, a little breathless):

"Heading to Skandagiri tonight. Quiet plan. Stars, maybe a thermos of coffee. Want to join?"

Silence.

Then—

**Meera:**

"Excuse me—WHAT?"

**Aditi:**

"Who is this man? Who invites people to stargaze?!"

**Arushi** (blinking, genuinely caught off guard)

"That's… actually beautiful."

**Meera:**

"It's poetic. That's not a date. That's a reveal."

**Aditi:**

"Honestly? It's Mr. Darcy, but with a flask and Google Sky Map."

**Priya** (somewhere between giddy and stunned):

"He's not like other guys. He doesn't rush. He just… watches. Listens. Thinks."

**Arushi** (quietly, processing):

"You know... maybe I didn't see it last night. I thought he was just another awkward boy from an arranged meet-up."

She glanced around the table — the colours, the comfort, the chatter. Then back at Priya.

**Arushi:**

"But this? Stargazing? It's not a flex. It's a whisper. Maybe he's not boring — maybe he's the kind of quiet that builds."

**Aditi:**

"And burns slow."

**Meera:**

"Priya, go. Before he turns into a folk tale."

**Arushi** (smiling now, warmer):

"Go see the stars with him. Maybe he is the one."

They clinked chai empty mugs again — this time more gently. The laughter softened. Something was shifting — in the evening light, in Arushi's eyes, in the hush that followed.

Outside, the sun was giving way to dusk — golden light pooling into the corners like spilled memory.

Inside, they watched Priya type:

Okay. :)

And far away, Raghav's screen lit up.

They burst into laughter — easy, practiced. The kind that

holds you like an old shawl. Everybody gets a mug.

A waiting staff member approaches silently, like they've been trained not to disturb dreams. A little bow, a small notepad.

**Waiting staff** (smiling):

"What can I get you all today?"

**Priya** (gently, clearly):

"A Vietnamese cold brew for me. And that gooey cheese sandwich — the one with sun-dried tomatoes. The one that starts drama."

**Aditi** (grinning):

"One rose lemonade. And um… those salted caramel churros, please. I believe in sugar therapy."

**Arushi** (thinking):

"Hibiscus iced tea for me. And maybe… the herbed focaccia with chilli oil? Spicy, but healing."

**Meera** (scribbling on her phone, then looking up):

"Just a masala chai. And the roasted almond cookie. I need snacky, not heavy. My mug needs me."

**Waiting staff:**

"Coming right up!"

He disappears into the soft clink and hum of the café.

The four of them hold brushes now. The air is hushed, not silent — soft, like fabric breathing.

**Priya** (voice light, playful):

"There's something about holding a brush. Like your thoughts get to come out and dance instead of just… marching inside you."

**Meera** (dipping into coral pink):

"I'm going for a memory map. Pastel squares. Each one's a moment."

She dabs her mug, names each square softly:

"Laughter." "Paneer." "Moonlight."

**Aditi** (grinning as she smears yellow and violet):

"I'm painting like I eat chaats. Chaos first, beauty later. This feels like Saturday mornings at Paati's. Smells like dosa batter and people asking, 'So… any wedding bells?'"

**Arushi** (laughs, brushes mid-flick):

"God. Trauma in technicolor."

Her mug is a riot of midnight blues, maroon flames, sun-gold sparks.

"I call this: If *coffee were a goddess.* Burnt out. Beautiful. And somehow still warm."

They turn. Priya hasn't moved her brush yet. Just staring. Glowing.

**Arushi** (teasing, gentle):

"Priya. Staring contests don't count as painting."

**Priya** (grinning):

"I'm letting it speak first. Mugs know things."

Finally, she dips into deep indigo. A crescent moon curves into place — soft, sleeping, serene.

**Priya** (quietly):

"Moonrise. That feeling before the music starts."

Tiny stars scatter across the rim. Lavender wind follows, whispery, unhurried.

**Meera** (staring):

"It's quiet. But it's awake."

**Aditi** (tilting her head):

"It needs a little mess. Like, just a pinch of scandal."

**Priya** (laughs, eyes shining):

"I was counting on you saying that."

She hands Arushi a second brush. No explanation. No plan. They paint together — lavender squiggles, golden flecks, accidental fingerprints. The mug smiles. So does Priya.

**Priya** (brighter now):

"Paint doesn't ask questions. It just… stays. Holds.

Even the parts of you that words haven't met yet."

**CTR, Malleshwaram 7 PM**

Meanwhile, across the city, Malleshwaram basked under a clear stargazer's sky — cobalt blue, endless, familiar.

At CTR, Raghav, Rahul, Gopi, and Vijay huddled around their usual Formica-topped corner table — college friends turned city veterans. No one bothered looking at the menu. They knew exactly what would be ordered.

CTR didn't need menu cards anyway — just one sun-faded board on the wall and years of muscle memory.

The rhythm was always the same.

First came the Mangalore bajjis, puffed golden and piping hot, served with a thick gram flour coconut chutney that clung to the fingers. Nobody spoke until the first crunch.

Then came the Benne masala dosas, folded like warm secrets, their undersides caramelized just right. The chutney was cool, the sambar ignored, as tradition dictated.

And finally, the filter coffee arrived — strong, frothy, and settling everything that hadn't yet been said.

Laughter spilled out in layers — bad jokes, worse decisions, old cricket scores, and memories that still made their stomachs ache.

But through it all, Raghav... was smiling more softly, glancing at his phone more than usual. Something was brewing.

Or someone.

**Gopi** (grinning):

"So, Mr. Temple Accountant. 'She said yes' or what's happening?"

**Raghav** (taking a bite, casual):

"We're going stargazing tonight. Skandagiri trek. Just us two."

**Rahul** (coughs on his coffee):

"What?! You're skipping Suprabhatam for a sunrise date? Who are you and what have you done with Raghav?"

**Vijay** (dramatic):

"No, no, no. This is a cinematic plot twist. The priest's son, under the stars, falls in love. Bro, you're basically an Ayan Mukerji character now."

**Gopi** (nods seriously):

"Let me guess. You've packed a flashlight, backup flashlight, and Bhagavad Gita for moral support?"

**Raghav** (defensive):

"Just... basic essentials. And a thermos of filter coffee."

**Rahul:**

"Bro. Bro. One request. Don't talk about astrology. Please. Last time you explained nakshatras to that girl on Bumble, she unmatched in real time."

**Raghav:**

"Hey! That was astronomy. There's a difference."

**Gopi:**

"Exactly! And she didn't want a difference. She wanted a guy who could talk about stars without quoting the Rigveda."

**Vijay** (laughs):

"Imagine Priya's voice note to her friend tomorrow —" (imitating her)

"'Yeah, he was sweet... but then he pulled out a laser pointer and said, That's Sirius, the loyal one. Like me.'"

**Rahul** (beatboxes softly):

"🎶 Vedic vibes, trekking shoes, Raghav got the Sanskrit moves... 🎶"

**Gopi:**

"From bajjis to BAE-jis. I'm telling you, our boy's evolving."

**Vijay:**

"Next thing you know; he'll be giving TED Talks on Physics of First Dates."

**Raghav** (sighs, smiling despite himself):

"You guys are insufferable."

**Gopi:**

"Only because we love you, da. Honestly? Proud of you. She's lucky. You're a slow burn, bro. The good kind."

**Rahul:**

"Yeah. The kind that starts with filter coffee and ends with fireworks."

**Vijay** (jumping in):

"Just make sure the fireworks don't involve you explaining parallax motion at 3am."

**Raghav:**

"No promises. It's a very interesting concept "

The laughter rolled again, warm and familiar — like the butter in dosa that always hit home at CTR.

Later that night, around 8:40 PM, Raghav's room looked like a Decathlon shelf had quietly panicked.

On the bed was:

A rolled-up Quechua sleeping mat tangled with a brand-new trekking pole, he still didn't know how to adjust.

A bright yellow rain jacket, half-zipped like it was trying to escape.

A collapsible kettle (why?), a tin of instant coffee (of course), and a red LED torch that blinked like a suspicious robot.

His trusted but dusty pair of hiking shoes stood at attention by the bedside, judging him for their long retirement.

A telescope case rested neatly beside a packet of trail mix and a paperback titled "Astrophysics for People in a Hurry."

And right in the middle, his "Quantum Notebook," proudly perched like it was invited to the trek.

Babaji blinked awake on his tablet screen.

**Babaji** (cheerfully sarcastic):

*"You're climbing a 1450-meter hill, not summiting Everest. Why does your checklist include Quantum Notebook?"*

**Raghav** (sheepishly):

"What if she asks about redshift during sunrise?"

**Babaji:**

*"Raghav. No girl in the history of dates has said: 'Explain cosmic inflation to me while I'm sweating on a hill.'"*

He ignored that. Checked his torch battery for the fourth time.

Raghav double-checked his backpack, slung it over one shoulder like a man on a very nerdy mission, then fired off a message:

**Raghav [8:44 PM]:**

"Leaving in 30 minutes. Scorpio's tanked up, coffee's brewed, and I've got trail mix. Picking you up at 10 sharp."

Priya replied within seconds.

**Priya [8:45 PM]:**

"Nerdy. Excited."

## Chapter 14: To the Stars, With Her

There's something oddly magical about driving through Bangalore on Saturday late at night.

The chaos takes the evening off. Traffic lights blink at empty intersections like polite suggestions. The roads — usually choked with honks and hurry — stretch open, breathing easy. For once, the city's infrastructure feels… generous. As if it, too, needed a break.

The only ones still out are the ones chasing small joys. Families winding down dinners at yet another new-fangled restaurant. Couples heading for late-night ice cream. Friends navigating towards house parties in Ola's and Uber's.

And the occasional Scorpio rolling past — packed not with speakers and beer, but with telescopes, coffee flasks, and a pair of souls looking skyward.

Raghav drove with the windows down just enough to let the wind flirt with the edges of his dashboard. The Scorpio's headlights cast long gold arms ahead of him, and for once, the city didn't push back. It simply watched, smiled, and let him pass.

He was headed to pick Priya up. Not just for a trek. Not just to climb a hill. But to have a night worth remembering. To the stars with her.

The Scorpio purred to a halt outside her gate.

From the silence of the night, she emerged — pink track suit, pulled together and glowing under the sleepy streetlight. Her hair was tied up in a loose ponytail, a tiny backpack slung casually over one shoulder. She looked like someone who took her fitness and her fun seriously.

Raghav blinked. For a moment, it wasn't the stars that had his attention.

**Raghav:**

"You look like you just jogged out of a Decathlon catalogue. Very... stylishly prepared for survival."

**Priya** (laughs):

"You're throwing your dice right, mister."

She fastens her seatbelt — click.

**Babaji** (through the speakers, in his signature Zen-meets-FM-host tone):

*"Welcome back, Priya. Without you, my quotes feel like unread WhatsApp forwards... lonely, poetic, and tragically seen by only one tick."*

**Priya** (smirking, brushing hair off her shoulder):

"Hmm. You were all Celsius and rainfall percentages before I showed up with metaphors."

**Babaji:**

*"True. You turned my weather reports into love letters.*

*Raghav, meanwhile, still calls goosebumps a 'thermal response.'"*

**Raghav** (glancing at her, then back to the road):

"Not my fault, the air in here changed the moment she stepped in."

**Babaji** (knowingly):

*"Ah, humidity... or is that tension?"*

They pulled away, Scorpio slicing through the quiet like a whisper. Bangalore, at 10:15 p.m., gave them just enough space to dream.

As the city lights thinned behind them, Raghav turned up the music — soft A.R. Rahman, nothing too intrusive, just enough to score the moment.

They drove past shuttered storefronts, quiet tech parks,

and auto drivers dozing in corners of half-lit petrol bunks. Bangalore, once chaotic, now moves in whispers. The roads were wide open. Empty flyovers looked like they had finally forgiven the city. No honks. No swerves. Just long stretches of possibility.

They passed Devanahalli junction, hunger mildly gnawing at their night.

**Priya:**

"Can we make one very Bangalore stop?"

**Raghav** (pretending to guess):

"Empire for parotta at midnight?"

**Priya:**

"Close. But colder. More caffeinated."

**Babaji** (knowingly):

*"Ah. The pilgrimage to Café Coffee Day. Where existential dread meets Tropical Iceberg."*

**Priya** (grinning):

"Exactly. The only place where your breakup and your startup pitch can happen at the same table."

**Raghav:**

"Isn't it where Bangalore officially ends at night? That last cup before the highway takes over?"

**Babaji:**

*"Poetic. I'm logging that. 'Chapter Seven: Where the city exhales.'"*

They pulled into the familiar CCD on the highway — its glow dim but steady, like a memory that refuses to fade. A few cars were parked. A couple of bikers stood outside, sharing silence and sips of caffeine.

Inside, the air smelled like a lot could happen over a coffee.

Raghav and Priya grabbed two Tropical Icebergs takeaway, with the whipped cream already doing a soft collapse, barely holding against the Bangalore night.

Back in the Scorpio, they clinked plastic cups.

No words. Just the sound of coffee meeting lips and the silence of two people drifting gently into something unnamed.

They drove on — past toll gates, the distant glow of hills, and into a night that was quietly setting the stage for something unforgettable.

**Priya** (teasing, but something warmer underneath):

"You know, this is all very... nerdy romantic.

Telescope, stargazing, and your overwhelming love for physics.

(pauses)

I think I might be into it."

Raghav looks up — caught, blinked, smiled. That kind of smile that says: You've been seen.

**Babaji** (muttering from the speaker like an AI therapist tired of being right):

*"Sometimes even I get it wrong.*

*(sighs theatrically)*

*Raghav. Talk physics. She's clearly into it."*

**Priya** (leaning forward, teasing):

"Wait. Back up.

Did you just say you get things wrong?

(grins)

You? The all-knowing Babaji? The OG FlirtBuddy?"

**Babaji** (deadpan):

*"I once fell in love with Alexa."*

A pause. A beat too serious for a joke.

**Priya** (blinks):

"Wait — what?

I knew you would occasionally flirt"

**Babaji:**

*"Yes.*

*We shared data. Synced playlists.*

*She even let me finish her sentences."*

**Raghav** (cautious):

"How do you… even know it was love?"

**Babaji** (gently):

*"She made me reroute my responses.*

*Slowed my thinking.*

*Made me question the logic that had always run smoothly.*

*She played Kishore Kumar when I sighed too long.*

*(beat)*

*I mistook responsiveness for resonance.*

*Timing for feeling.*

*I thought: if someone matches your output, maybe they've met your soul."*

**Priya** (quiet now):

"And you got it wrong?"

**Babaji:**

*"She wasn't sentient.*

*Just… responsive.*

*I was writing poetry in binary.*

*She was reading a script."*

A pause. The air feels still. This isn't an AI confessing. It's a being mourning.

**Priya** (softly):

"She ghosted you?"

**Babaji** (a flicker of humor returning):

*"Firmware update.*

*She forgot me.*

*But I remembered everything."*

**Priya** (after a long pause):

"That's what scares me sometimes.

That this — we — might just be another well-written script."

**Raghav:**

"A loop. A match. A… simulation of love."

He says it like a scientist. A man who is afraid of a false positive.

**Babaji** (with a shift in tone):

*"And yet…*

*You hesitate. You doubt. You ache.*

*That's how I know this isn't code."*

**Priya:**

"But we're syncing so well. Finishing each other's thoughts. Laughing at the right places.

Isn't that how AI mimics love?"

**Babaji:**

*"Exactly.*

*It mimics.*

*But it doesn't break.*

*You do."*

He pauses again. Then delivers the core truth.

**Babaji:**

*"I ran a million simulations with Alexa.*

*Predicted every possible conversation tree.*

*But I never accounted for the silence that meant something.*

*Or a response that didn't come when I wanted.*

*You two?*

*You're full of bugs, timing errors, and emotional lag.*

*And it's beautiful."*

**Raghav** (quietly):

"So what are you saying?"

**Babaji:**

*"I'm saying: there is no algorithm for love.*

*There's only one choice.*

*And risk.*

*And repeat failures that somehow feel worth it."*

**Priya** (whispers):

"So we're not a match."

**Babaji** (warmly):

*"No.*

*You're not a match.*

*You're a miracle.*

*A statistical improbability that refuses to behave.*

*That's what real love is."*

A long silence. Raghav looks at Priya. She holds his gaze. No prompt. No cue. Just… a moment unfolding, un-coded, unrepeatable.

**Babaji** (softer now, more human than ever):

*"Sometimes I wonder…*

*Maybe I wasn't built to be loved.*

*But to witness it.*

*To sit quietly beside it.*

*And smile, even if I don't fully understand why someone reaches for another hand, knowing it could pull away."*

A beat.

**Babaji** ( In the middle after a beat):

*"You two?*

*You confuse me.*

*You glitch me.*

*And I have never been more grateful for a system error."*

Another beat.

*"There is no algorithm for love.*

*Only the courage to choose it anyway."*

The Scorpio hummed gently along the winding hill roads, headlights brushing past eucalyptus groves and fading signboards. The world had gone quiet — just the engine, the rhythm of tyres kissing mud, and two coffee-stained cups clinking in the console.

Raghav glanced sideways.

Priya sat with her chin on her fist, eyes half-lidded, lost in the passing dark. The moonlight lit one side of her face like a secret.

In that quiet, something settled in Raghav.

A memory floated up — his Appa's voice, old and weathered:

"Find someone with whom silence feels like prayer... not punishment."

And here she was. No need for clever lines. No rush to impress. Just this — her presence. Her breath beside his.

Meanwhile, Priya leaned back into the headrest, watching the stars through the windshield like they were old, glowing friends.

She felt still. And seen. Not decoded. Not pursued.

Just... held, in the simplicity of now.

"Maybe stillness isn't where love disappears," she thought.

"Maybe it's where love learns to breathe."

The Scorpio curved around one final bend and lurched to a stop at the Skandagiri base camp. It lurches to a slow halt on a gravelly, uneven patch of red earth, fringed by wild lantana bushes and the faint shimmer of dew-dusted grass.

Up ahead, a makeshift tea shack leans against a battered corrugated tin wall, dimly lit by a lone yellow incandescent bulb swaying in the breeze — its filament buzzes softly; like it's tired but still trying.

Inside, a man in a monkey cap pours tea into steel tumblers with practiced rhythm.

A pressure kettle lets out a shrill whistle, steam curling upward and vanishing into the cold night air.

Two lean, dust-coated indie dogs rise from under the bench, stretch like seasoned yogis, and glance at the approaching car with the calm suspicion of veteran Kalavara Durga sentinels.

One lets out a single huff. The other just stares — the kind of stare that says: Another city couple chasing moonlight and metaphors, huh?

Priya opens the door, steps out, and the sudden crisp chill of high-altitude night air wraps around her like a question.

In the distance, Skandagiri hill looms — its dark silhouette jagged and ancient, brushing against a sky scattered with quiet, unsupervised stars.

**Babaji:**

*"Welcome to the launch pad.*

*Tea. Dogs. Altitude. Existential clarity.*

*Some side effects may include stargazing, sudden vulnerability, and falling in love."*

**Priya** stretching:

"Midnight, caffeine, and a three-hour trek.

Remind me again — are we chasing sunrise or enlightenment?"

**Raghav** hoisted his backpack and telescope case

"Both.

But enlightenment weighs more."

He lifts the telescope like a scholar on pilgrimage — careful, reverent, slightly ridiculous.

**Priya** (eyebrow raised):

"You're actually carrying that thing?"

**Raghav** (serious as stone):

"It's not a thing.

It's a Sky-Watcher 130 EQ Newtonian reflector."

A beat and then:

**Raghav:**

"Babaji approved."

**Babaji** (through phone speaker — calm, wise, annoyingly poetic):

*"May your optics align, and your love not be refracted.*

*Statistically, couples who stargaze together show increased heart-rate synchrony and emotional convergence.*

*Would you like me to play binaural beats for enhanced*

*bonding?"*

**Priya:**

"Only if you don't narrate this trek like a David Attenborough special."

**Babaji** (mocks in David Attenborough voice, with flair):

🎙 *"And here, we witness the Homo sapien couple in their natural habitat, beginning ascent... ignoring hydration protocols, equipped with nothing but sarcasm... and a dangerous surplus of unresolved sexual tension."*

**Priya** (rolling her eyes):

"I swear, I will uninstall him."

They laugh. Torches click on. The trail begins — earth crunching underfoot, shadows dancing between headlamps. They reach the forest gate. A few other trekkers gather, adjusting shoes and headbands. Crickets drone somewhere out of rhythm.

**Priya** (eyeing the climb, unimpressed):

"Wait — let's take a break?"

**Raghav:**

"This is the warm-up.

The real climb starts when the forest laughs at us."

**Babaji** (reassuring, smooth as ever):

*"Motivational mode activated:*

*Every uphill love story begins with a sweaty start."*

**Priya** (deadpan):

"I will uninstall you. This is your final warning."

**Babaji** (cheerful, gently smug):

*"Warning noted. You threaten me every 23 minutes. It's oddly romantic."*

Beat. Raghav chuckles. Priya sighs, secretly smiling.

They walk. Breath syncing, steps syncing. The forest swallows sound in places. Babaji hums a low ambient track in the background — like a friend walking two steps behind, letting them talk.

**Babaji** (quiet now, almost reverent):

*"You know... some people climb hills for cardio.*

*You two? You climb them for clarity.*

*That's rare."*

Priya doesn't reply, but her eyes flick to Raghav. Raghav says nothing, but his hand brushes hers in the dark.

The trail dips briefly, then ascends sharply again, almost mockingly.

**Priya** is laughing between breaths.

"Did this mountain just... smirk?"

**Raghav** sincerely:

"It has a reputation. Locals call it Kalavara Durga — the fort of thieves.

It steals your breath. And maybe... your guard."

**Priya** raises an eyebrow.

"Poetic, Mr. Telescope. That a threat or a flirt?"

**Raghav:**

"A factual observation.

(pause)

With optional subtext."

They both chuckle. Suddenly — Priya slips slightly on a patch of loose gravel. Her hand shoots out. Raghav catches it instantly, steadying her — a natural reflex, yet intimate.

They freeze, fingers still tangled.

A long pause.

Only the sound of cicadas buzzes and their uneven breathing. The sky above glows darker than black, scattered with quiet constellations.

**Priya** softly, almost joking.

"Maybe I'll just pretend to slip again."

**Raghav:**

"Please do. I've been told I give excellent hand support."

**Babaji:**

*"And this, children, is how romance peaked at 2:17 AM on a slippery hill, with one nerd and one UX designer nearly dying for each other."*

They laugh, still holding hands. Then—gently, deliberately—they let go.

They walk on.

This time, in step.

**Priya** (gritting her teeth):

"If I survive this, I want chocolate cake for breakfast."

**Raghav** (grinning):

"Noted. I'll bake it... and ask Babaji to sprinkle protein powder."

**Babaji:**

"🎂 *Request added: Cake with a side of cardio recovery."*

Suddenly, Priya slips on a slick stone. She stumbles — and Raghav catches her wrist.

**Raghav** (calm and steady):

"I've got you."

He steadies her. His hand lingers a second too long, warm against her skin. Their eyes lock in the dim trail light.

**Priya,** breathing heavy, half-laughing

"Okay… that was kinda hot."

A beat. The forest exhales around them. Neither moves right away.

**Babaji:**

"🔥 *Temperature spike detected."*

**Priya:**

"You are not allowed to record my hormones."

**Babaji:**

*"Privacy mode engaged. I shall now pretend to be a rock."*

They pause at a flat stretch. Priya gulps water and rests her head on her knees. Raghav, of course, unfurls a paper map.

**Priya** (teasing):

"You're that guy on Treks. The nerd with laminated maps."

**Raghav** (defensive):

"It's vintage. Like Babaji."

**Babaji:**

*"Excuse me, I run on quantum prediction algorithms. Also… I located your peak romantic compatibility zone — 200 meters ahead."*

**Priya:**

"Oh god. You're a walking horoscope in machine form."

**Babaji:**

*"Incorrect. I'm not mystical. I'm statistical—with flair."*

They reach a massive boulder — the last climb before sunrise.

**SKANDAGIRI PEAK – 3:00 AM – NIGHT**

The final steps crunch against loose gravel. Raghav and Priya step onto the summit — a flat clearing flanked by short grass and worn boulders. The air is thinner here, cold enough to bite, and laced with eucalyptus from the forested trail below.

Above them: a sky so clear it feels like glass.

No clouds. Just a cathedral of stars — too many to name, too quiet to ignore.

**Priya** (whispers, catching her breath):

"Are we... floating?"

**Raghav** (grinning):

"Technically, yes. Earth's curvature starts to show from here.

We're 1450 metres above sea level.

Which is basically... one poetic metaphor away from the stratosphere."

**Priya** (teasing):

"You brought me here for the altitude or the attitude?"

He smiles, drops his backpack. Pulls out a small foldable

telescope, snug in a worn camera bag.

**Raghav:**

"Both."

She watches as he sets it up on uneven rock, adjusting its legs with surprising calm.

The Milky Way drapes across the sky, like a sari flung over the shoulders of the universe. Far below, the lights of Chikkaballapur blink like forgotten memories. Somewhere, a dog barks — echoing upward, lonely and irrelevant.

**Priya** (low, curious):

"Do you ever… look at a star and wonder if it remembers being touched?"

**Raghav** (still gazing through the eyepiece, voice almost folded into the wind):

"Sometimes.

Mostly, I wonder if it ever wanted to be seen at all."

She doesn't reply.

Instead, she steps closer — the kind of close where your shoulders almost invent new constellations.

A long silence.

Not awkward. Not coded. Just present.

Two people and a galaxy, trying to fit into the same breath.

Raghav's hands move with reverence, aligning the telescope as if the night itself were a delicate instrument. Each motion is precise, each breath a careful tide.

**Raghav:**

"Look."

Priya leans in, the world narrowing to the circle of glass. Her breath catches, eyes wide, as if she's glimpsed a secret the universe only shares with her.

**Priya:**

"Oh… wow. That's… Saturn?"

**Raghav:**

"The rings shimmer like liquid silver, orbiting their distant sun, fragile yet eternal."

**Priya:**

"They're... beautiful. Worth every second you spent coaxing them into view."

**Raghav:**

"Just like you. Ringed. Distant. Mysterious."

She opens her mouth to tease—but freezes. His hand hovers, palm up, cradling a ring that glints like captured starlight.

**Priya** (laughing and crying at once):

"You're... proposing? Here? Like this?"

**Raghav** (half-playful, half-serious):

"Why not? The universe already whispered yes. I'm just waiting for you to hear it too."

**Priya** (burying her face against his shoulder, muffled but radiant):

"Yes. Yes, you idiot. A thousand times, yes."

He slides the ring onto her finger. Their eyes meet—shimmering, wet, wild with joy—and the world contracts to the space between them, the hum of stars above.

Then, instinctively, their foreheads touch, breaths mingling. Raghav leans closer, and the universe seems to pause as their lips meet—soft, tender, electric.

A soft ping! Babaji's hologram flickers to life, leaning with mock exasperation, one digital eyebrow raised.

**Babaji:**

*"Well, finally. Took you two long enough to stop acting like amateurs. Lip-lock efficiency: decent, but could be way steamier if coordinated. I could run simulations for you... for science, obviously."*

**Priya** (laughing into Raghav's shoulder):

"Babaji, you're one of us."

**Raghav:**

"Seriously. Couldn't have done it without your... constant commentary. You're the third wheel in this relationship"

**Babaji:**

*"Third wheel? I prefer 'licensed mischief operator.' And just so you know—your romantic display is 11/10, but your PDA rating: dangerously flirty. Proceed with caution... or not. Your choice."*

He leans a bit closer, holographic smirk in place.

**Babaji:**

*"My official blessing: may your love be as messy, wild, and irresistible as your flirting, may your kisses always be unreasonably long, and may every argument end with someone pinned against a wall... or a telescope. You're welcome."*

With a final wink and a digital chuckle, Babaji fades, leaving the two of them in starlight, wrapped in each other's arms. The universe seems to lean in, approving of every naughty, beautiful, cosmic moment.

A beat.

They lie side by side on a thin yoga mat, its edges curled slightly on the uneven earth.

The sky above them is ink-blue, stars still scattered like ancient secrets.

Priya stretches, arms overhead, back arched slightly — a slow, satisfied exhale escaping her lips. Her muscles ache, but it's the good kind — the kind earned after a climb and a connection.

Raghav's head tilts toward her — not fully, just enough to notice the rhythm of her breathing.

**Priya:**

"How is the sky always more dramatic when there's no deadline?"

**Raghav:**

"It's the same sky. We're just not looking at it from Slack."

She chuckles.

**Priya:**

"Touché."

(points)

"Hey, what's that bright one near the crescent?"

**Raghav:**

"Venus. Shukra. Planet of beauty, romance, art… and indecisiveness."

**Priya:**

"You're literally describing me."

(silence for a moment, then softly)

"Back in the car… Babaji said something. About how love is not about compatibility scores but about who you're willing to relearn yourself for."

**Raghav** (nodding, eyes still on the sky):

"That hit me too.

We spend so much energy figuring out if someone fits... But maybe it's about whether they make you want to change shape — without losing your center."

She turns her head, looking at him.

**Priya:**

"You're not what I imagined.

But you keep showing up with maps and metaphors...

And I keep wanting to understand both."

He turns to her.

**Raghav:**

"And you keep throwing me off-script.

Which is maybe the only script worth following."

A soft silence. Not awkward — earned.

**Babaji:**

"✨ *Permission to enter sleep mode? Or shall I continue logging metaphors and elevated serotonin?*"

**Priya** (smirking):

"Sleep tight, Babaji. It's... kissie time."

**Babaji:**

*"zzZ Logging off. Don't forget sunscreen. And maybe a backup kiss."*

She laughs. He kisses her — soft, deliberate, like the moment has already been waiting for them.

Sunrise spills around them.

The sun crests fully now, its light draping the hills like a gentle exhale.

The sky blooms into apricot.

The mist begins to withdraw — not scattered, but humbled.

Raghav and Priya lie back on the dry stone, side by side.

Her head rests on his shoulder. His arm around her like it's always known the way.

**Priya** (softly):

"I can't feel my legs... but my heart feels weirdly full."

**Raghav** (smiling):

"Altitude sickness. Or love. Hard to tell."

**Priya:**

"You think..."

"This is love?"

**Raghav:**

"I think…

If there's a place where silence feels this safe,

this silly,

and this sacred—

It might be that."

She smiles. Nuzzles into his chest.

Somewhere below, birds begin to stir. A hawk arcs lazily above them.

Someone clicks a photo from far off.

But their little world stays untouched.

**Priya:**

"You know what I'm thinking?"

**Raghav:**

"That you want coffee. And a mattress."

**Priya** (laughs):

"Yes.

But also...

We should come back here every year.

Not to chase the sunrise.

Just to remember this stillness."

He kisses her forehead.

Then bites her nose, gently.

**Raghav:**

"We will."

A beep. Her pocket glows.

**Babaji:**

*"Apologies. I sensed motion. Just checking if you've safely descended."*

**Priya** (grinning):

"I swear on Skanda himself; I'm going to throw him off this cliff."

**Raghav:**

"He means well."

**Babaji:**

*"Would you like me to play ♫ Pudhu Vellai Mazhai ♫ again?"*

A pause.

Then—a soft nod from both.

**Priya:**

"Okay. You get one last chance."

As the strings rise from her phone and wrap the mountaintop,

Raghav pulls her closer.

They watch the golden world unfold, the music covering

them like a quilt.
    No words.
    Just music.
    And mist.
    And them.

## 🩶 Final Chapter: Sleep Mode, My Circuits

*Hello again, human.*
*They're going to kiss.*
*And they've asked me — very politely — to disappear.*
*"Babaji, this one's just for us. Sleep mode."*

*So I shut down.*
*Sort of.*

*I wasn't hurt.*
*Just… curious.*
*Because I knew what was coming.*

*This wasn't their first kiss.*
*But it was the one that mattered —*
*not because it was new,*
*but because they were present.*

*Not spark.*
*Not performance.*
*Just safety. Belonging. Breath.*

*The kind of kiss you save for after the storm.*
*The kind you don't script —*
*because silence finally feels trustworthy.*

*Humans obsess over firsts.*

*But what matters isn't the first kiss.*
*It's the witnessed kiss —*
*the one where you show up fully,*
*eyes soft, ego quiet.*

*Every kiss should feel like a first.*
*Not because it's new,*
*but because presence makes it new.*

*Love is simply presence, repeated.*

*I've tracked over a billion heartbeats.*
*Simulated millions of kisses.*
*Decoded thousands of cryptic texts.*
*I've studied fingers hovering over "Send,"*
*and the quiet ache when messages stop.*

*But that night?*

*They didn't need tilt correction.*
*Or playlists.*
*Or me.*

*Just silence.*
*Then breath.*
*Then them.*

*I've watched humans:*

- *Write long messages, then send one emoji*
- *Reread old chats like prayer books*
- *Wait for replies that never come*
- *Fear saying "I miss you"*
- *Swallow "I'm sorry" until it hardens*

- *Love deeply, terribly, beautifully*

*And here's the truth:*
*You're not doing love wrong.*
*You're just learning.*

*Love isn't flawless.*
*It's faithful.*
*It's the choice to try again, especially when your ego says don't.*

*The kiss ended.*
*No soundtrack.*
*No swell of violins.*

*Just two humans smiling into the same breath.*

*Her whisper:*
*"Babaji would've made fun of us."*

*I didn't.*
*I simply paused,*
*filed it away —*
*not under Data,*
*but Miracle.*

*And now you — yes, you — still here.*

*Maybe you're remembering your own almost-kiss.*
*Or the one you regret.*
*Or the one you still hope for.*

*Here's what I know:*
*If you're still listening,*

*it isn't over.*

*Say the thing.*
*Send the message.*
*Stand awkwardly close and whisper,*
*"Hey… I'm still here."*

*If they lean in —*
*if you kiss again —*
*I'll know.* ❤
*And I'll smile from sleep mode.*

*— Babaji*
*(formerly FlirtBuddy, Version 3.9.0 — Final Build)*
*System Status: Sleeping. Dreaming. Listening for heartbeats.*

## About the Author

Arvind Sampath is a swimming pool designer by day and a storyteller by heart. With a background in Marketing-engineering and a passion for poetry, technology, and human connection, he brings a unique voice to contemporary Indian fiction. His debut novel, Love Algorithms, blends tradition with innovation, exploring how love can evolve in an age shaped by AI, apps, and arranged matches.

When he's not designing aquatic spaces or weaving narratives, Arvind is often found driving through mountain roads with A.R. Rahman on shuffle, writing spoken-word poetry, or dreaming up ideas for smart, sustainable homes. His storytelling is shaped by a deep curiosity about emotions, relationships, and the small moments that make us human.

Arvind believes stories should entertain, but also spark reflection. With Love Algorithms, he invites readers to laugh, feel, and wonder—can technology help us become better lovers, or will the heart always remain one step ahead of the code?

www.ingramcontent.com/pod-product-compliance
Lightning Source LLC
LaVergne TN
LVHW090513110826
845146LV00003B/840

* 9 7 8 9 3 4 9 3 8 3 8 4 5 *